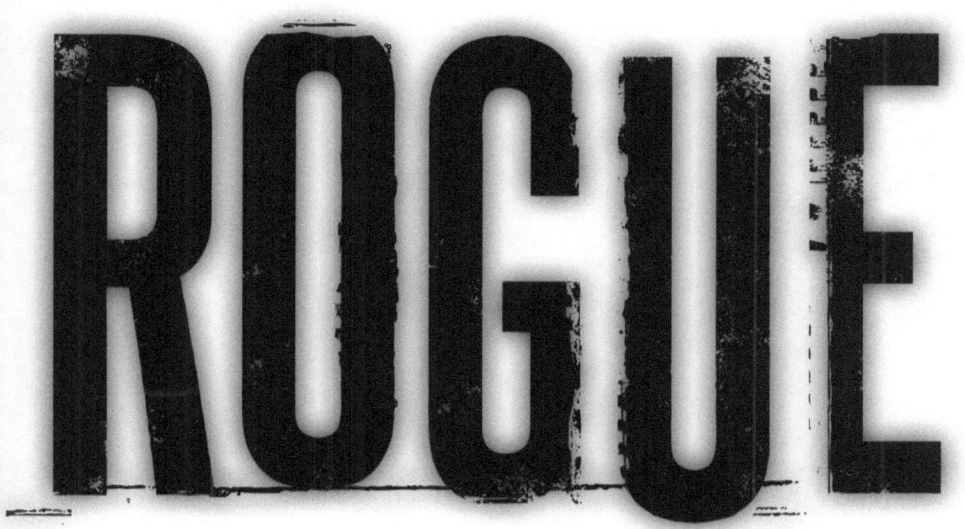

ROGUE

GREG F. GIFUNE

JOURNALSTONE
YOUR LINK TO ARTIST TALENT

JournalStone books may be ordered through booksellers or by contacting:

JournalStone

www.journalstone.com

ISBN: 978-1-947654-53-2 (sc)
ISBN: 978-1-947654-54-9 (ebook)

JournalStone rev. date: September 14, 2018
2nd Edition

Library of Congress Control Number: 2018950978

Printed in the United States of America

Cover Design: Mikio Murakami
Interior Layout: Jess Landry

Proofread by Sean Leonard

ROGUE

For The Man From Another Place.

ROGUE:
A solitary animal of vicious character that has separated
from the herd.

"What matters isn't whether something is real.
What matters is if it's true."
—Jane Mendelsohn, Innocence

CHAPTER ONE

The light through the trees, that's what I remember most, that beautiful golden light. Like birth, I thought at the time, the start of something new, or perhaps the last memory of something old. Or just maybe, it was neither of those things, but a dream instead, a wonderful dream whispering what might be, what could be, what *will* be if only I'd believe.

And then just like that, I'm losing my mind. There are things in my head I can't get out. Not memories exactly, but similar things that remind me I'm slowly slipping into madness. I've figured out how to hang on enough to function, to fake my way through things and appear as if I'm fine. Only I'm not fine. I'm nowhere near fine. Like a cocoon, it encompasses me, and the tighter it wraps itself around what's left of me, the stronger it becomes. Despite my terror, and the terrible things nesting in my diseased brain, I've accepted the inevitable. I'm hanging on for dear life, but my grip is loosening. And there isn't a goddamn thing I can do about it. So there's no choice but to embrace the fall, because it's coming. It's coming with a vengeance.

Go ahead then. Take me.

And together, through eyes broken and bloodied, we'll see...

Am I dreaming? The nightmares don't stop anymore, so it's hard to tell. They quiet down now and then, but they're always here. Screeching in my head, the constant din echoes through my skull like the deafening clamor of giant invisible machines. Makes it difficult to tell where the world of shadows ends and reality begins.

Sometimes I wonder if there's a difference anymore. Maybe there never was.

Winter is coming soon. The trees are long bare, the air is sharp and clean, and gray skies typical of the season have already arrived. The world often seems unnaturally, eerily still this time of year, as if in frozen anticipation of things inconceivably profound. Days are shorter, the nights longer and more imposing and laced with the same uneasy silence. But it's the early morning hours, when it is neither day nor night but somewhere in between, that are particularly curious.

I step out onto my back deck, lean against the railing and sip my coffee. Bewildered, I find myself stranded in that strange chasm between restlessness and sleep, where conscious thought and unrestrained dreams are often indistinguishable. I'd been awakened by the distant though piercing and incessant wail of a car alarm, the same one that has awakened me several days in a row now. It comes from somewhere beyond our backyard. If one were to hop the fence and walk through the half mile or so of forest on the other side, one would eventually come out on a residential street far more populated than our quiet dead-end road, so it could've been coming from any number of vehicles. What is maddening is that it not only goes off each morning just before dawn, but after I roll out of bed, make my way downstairs, fix myself a cup of coffee and go out to the deck, it's always still wailing in the distance. Then it stops. Suddenly, just as it began.

As I lean against the railing and sip my coffee, my eyes follow the sound of the alarm to the fence and the woods beyond. And it is then that I see someone sitting in one of the Adirondack chairs that encircle the stone fire pit in the backyard. My heart stops a moment as my mind syncs up with my eyes. Am I really seeing someone there or is it a trick of the slowly strengthening light? I straighten my stance and squint in an attempt to bring the person into better focus, as the fire pit is more than thirty yards away. This is no illusion. A young man sits on the edge of one of the chairs, his elbows propped on his thighs and his head buried in his hands. I stand there and watch him awhile, unsure of what to do next.

After a quick visual sweep of the yard, I'm satisfied that he and I are alone. I put my mug on the deck table and pull my hooded sweatshirt in tight around me against the chill. In sweatpants and slippers, I slowly cross the yard toward the stranger.

I've nearly reached him when it occurs to me I don't even have a phone with me, and I regret not having called out to him from a greater distance before making my approach. I slow my pace and come to a stop on the far side of the fire pit. The man still hasn't moved and doesn't seem to know I'm there. I wonder, could I handle him physically if need be? Could I outrun him if I had to?

Finally, in a tone nonconfrontational but loud enough for him to hear me, I say: "Hello?"

The man slowly raises his head and looks over at me. He's significantly younger than I am—probably early twenties—and wears an expression of utter torment the level of which I've rarely encountered. His dark eyes are cheerless, brooding, bloodshot and saddled with black bags, his skin pale and drawn, his face covered in stubble, and he looks disheveled in a ratty pair of jeans, worn boots and a sweatshirt beneath a badly weathered brown leather jacket. He stares at me as if he's been waiting for me to arrive, but says nothing.

"Can I help you?" I ask.

He slowly shakes his head no.

I swallow hard but hope he hasn't noticed. "Are you all right?"

The young man wipes his eyes with the back of his hand. He's obviously been crying, and none-toogently.

"Has something happened?" I ask when he doesn't answer. "Can I help you in some way?"

"You think *you* can help *me*?" he asks, his voice a loud and raspy whisper.

"I don't know if I can, but—"

"You don't understand."

"Look, I live here." I clear my throat and stuff my hands in the pockets of my hoodie. "This is private property. I need to know why you're in my yard. If you're hurt or something's wrong or you need some help, I can…call someone for you or…"

The man reaches into the side pocket of his leather jacket and pulls out a pack of cigarettes and a lighter. Without looking at me, he stabs a cigarette between his lips, lights it, then exhales a stream of smoke at the fire pit. Though odd, there is nothing inherently intimidating about him, but he does have something of an edge to him. As another tear spills free and trickles the length of his face, he says, "There's nothing you can do, Cam. There's nothing anyone can do."

The sound of my name changes everything. "Do I know you?"

With a heavy sigh, he struggles to his feet.

Instinctually, I take a step back and away from him, but I continue to study his face. I'm certain I don't know this young man, have never seen or spoken to him before, and yet there's something vaguely familiar about him. "How do you know my name?" I ask. "Do we know each other?"

He smokes his cigarette, taking one angry pull after another, but doesn't answer.

"What are you doing back here?"

"I'm lost, I…"

Perhaps he's a mental patient or some poor soul off his medication. But neither option explains how he knows my name.

"Have we met before?" I press. "How do you know my name?"

"I know you," he says quietly, "but you don't know me. Not yet."

"I don't understand."

"Don't use the house phone. They're watching you."

Although I heard exactly what he said, I pretend I didn't. "I'm sorry?"

"They're watching you," he says, grimacing, "through the phone."

For some reason I feel compelled to look back over my shoulder at the house. It sits dark and quiet, offering nothing. Overhead, numerous phone wires run from the roof to a series of poles that lead back out to the street. I drive by or walk under them every day, and have done so for years. They've become so commonplace I rarely even notice them, yet now there seems something sinister and bizarre about them. How do objects that intrusive and unattractive ever manage to fade into the background?

"I don't know what you—" I turn back to him. "*Who's* watching me?"

"Something bad is going to happen."

I feel my gut tighten. "Are you threatening me?"

Brimming with tears, his sad eyes find mine. "I'm trying to help you."

Something deep within me insists I should believe him. "Who are you?"

The young man takes another drag on his cigarette, exhales through his nose, then flicks the butt into the fire pit. "I'm sorry. That's who I am."

He turns and walks toward the front yard. I call after him, ask him to wait and explain himself, but he acts as if he doesn't hear me. When he reaches the front yard, and the gate in the fence he must pass through to exit the property, he hesitates and looks back at me a moment.

Then he slips out through the gate and is gone.

* * *

Ours is a dead-end and relatively private street, a dirt road cut through a patch of forest in the small town of Sumner, Massachusetts. Besides our own, a modest colonial, there are only two other houses on Forest View Lane, one on either side of us. The last house on the street, a split-level cape, belongs to Bruce Deacon, a retired firefighter and widower whose wife Margaret died from a sudden heart attack two years ago. Bruce is an alcoholic. The other house has sat empty for more than a year. It's on the market, and now and then a real estate agent shows up with potential buyers and walks them through, but nothing ever comes of it.

A sudden tapping on the sliders behind me draws my attention away from the fence in the front yard. Remy stands on the other side of the slider looking at me quizzically, hair mussed and eyes still heavy with sleep. I cross the yard and return to the deck, scooping up my coffee as I pass by the table. "Morning," I say, stepping back into the house. "Coffee's on."

"Chilly out there." Remy hugs herself. "Why are you up so early?"

I close the slider. "That damn car alarm went off again."

"How do I sleep through it every time? Why were you out by the fire pit?"

"No reason." I don't know why I lie to her just then, but I do. "Just wanted to get some air, was taking a walk around the yard."

Remy rises up on her tiptoes, kisses me then shuffles off to the kitchen in her flannel pajamas, bright red numbers with little white penguins on them. An educated and strong woman, Remy can often be unconsciously childlike and vulnerable as well, a dichotomy I find not only fascinating, but often endearing.

Stifling a smile, I follow her into the kitchen. I stand there stupidly, staring at the wall phone as if I've seen a ghost.

Don't use the house phone.

Remy pours herself some coffee. "You were restless last night," she says softly.

They're watching you through the phone.

"Tossing and turning," she tells me, "that kind of thing."

"Sorry, did I keep you up?" I drink my coffee, notice the backyard through the window over the sink. Everything suddenly looks so stark out there.

"Worried about you, that's all. You kept moaning and groaning, sounded like you were in pain."

I force a smile I hope she believes. "Bad dreams, I guess."

"You okay?"

"Yeah," I lie again. "I started a new case yesterday. Read the file, looks like it's going to be particularly unpleasant, and that's saying something for my line of work."

She gives my shoulder a pat and offers up her best reassuring-though-still-half-asleep morning smile. "I'm going to put the news on real quick, then I need to get in the shower."

Like most people, Remy has no idea how I can do my job and remain sane. And like most people, she doesn't realize I can do no such thing, because I see a particular strain of human beings (for lack of a better term) at their worst on a daily basis. The fact that I work exclusively with those who hurt others, and often specifically target and victimize women and children, makes it even more difficult to comprehend. It's not unusual for me to discuss my cases with her, but I never do it in any detail, always using broad and general terms and glossing it over as best I can, as they're always horrific. Thing is, you can polish a turd all you like. You can work it until you see your reflection in the sonofabitch if it makes you (or someone else) feel any better, but at the end of the day, it's still a piece of shit. Maybe I do it to spare her, or maybe myself. Not sure it matters.

"Come on," Remy says, motioning to the great room, "let's go watch the news for a few, see what other wonderful things are happening across our lovely globe of endless peace and love."

"I need a refill," I say, holding my near-empty mug up as evidence. "Be right in."

When she leaves me alone in the kitchen, I feel oddly relieved. She doesn't know the troubles I've been having lately, not only in my personal life but also at work. I want to talk to her about it and have been trying to find a way and the right time to do so, but I'm afraid. And if whatever's happening to me scares me, then surely it will absolutely terrify her. Talking and commiserating with each other about our jobs is something all couples do, but her position as an English teacher, while a tough gig with its own set of challenges, hardly presents comparable issues to the ones I see every day. For years she's held the job at a private junior high school in a nearby town on Cape Cod, and while the pay isn't great, she's happy and fulfilled professionally, and that counts for something. Or it should. She's safe there. At least as safe as anyone can be today, which I suppose isn't very safe at all. But she doesn't have to deal with the things or people I do. She doesn't have to know the things I know. And that counts for something too.

How the hell did that kid know my name? I wonder. I know he's not one of my cases, but he could be connected to one of them somehow, and if that's it and he's come to my home, I have a major problem. Still baffled as to why I didn't tell Remy about it, I pour myself a fresh mug of coffee and notice my hands are shaking. That's been happening a lot lately too. Sometimes I can make it stop if I really concentrate. Most times I can't control it at all.

The furnace in the cellar kicks on, distracting me long enough to remember how outrageous the price of heating oil has become. Despite the chill in the house, I go to the den, find the thermostat and turn it down to sixty. The furnace falls silent. Waiting to see if Remy calls out an objection (she's always cold), I remain in the den, a small room off the kitchen where Remy and I often go to read or listen to music. In contrast to the great room, which sports a large HD television, framed vintage movie posters on the walls, a bar, a pool table and sliders leading to the deck, the den is an intimate, quiet room, Remy's favorite in the house, in fact. The walls are lined with book-cases, the shelves filled with paperbacks, hardbacks and numer-ous framed photographs chronicling our lives together over the years. Hardwood floors, a couch, coffee table and small stereo system in the corner round things out nicely.

As I take in the room, my eyes sweep to the window on the wall opposite the thermostat. There, through the pane of glass, is the empty house next door. A strange and uneasy feeling drifts through me.

I shiver. It feels as if the temperature in the room has plum-meted. But it simply isn't possible for the temperature to drop instantly.

I look beyond the empty house to the road.

No sign of the sad young man. He's out there somewhere, though.

And something tells me I haven't seen the last of him.

* * *

"This is really disturbing," Remy says. Curled up on the couch with her coffee, she frowns and nods at the television.

A local newscaster, who at first glance appears to be made entirely of wax, is talking about the government allegedly spy-ing on civilians. I only hear the tail end of the story, but since I work for the Commonwealth of Massachusetts, I'm always leery of conspiracy theories involving government. I know firsthand how dysfunctional it can be. On the other hand, I also know things are routinely swept under the proverbial rug or altered to suit the needs of those in charge or those in higher positions of authority, so government conspiracies aren't out of the question either. It's just that these things are usually execut-ed with such incompetence it's difficult to imagine a scenario where one might actually be effective.

"A former federal employee is alleging the government is not only listening in on phone calls and reading emails and texts between suspected terrorists or suspicious types in other countries," Remy explains, "but that they're doing it to everyone here in the U.S. too, regardless of who they are. They're just doing it with everyone and collecting these massive amounts of information on the population."

They're watching you through the phone.

"Seems hard to believe," I tell her, my heart suddenly racing.

She arches an eyebrow. "Does it?"

"That would have to be one hell of an undertaking, given the number of people, phones and computers in this country."

"But not impossible."

I shrug, feigning indifference. "Be nice if government was that efficient, but…"

"I don't know, Cam. Big Brother and all that, it's getting out of control. Privacy is becoming a thing of the past. We have the right to talk on our telephones or email and text without worrying about the government listening in on every conversation."

"Why would they care what you're talking about on the phone?"

"Not the point."

"Unless it has some bearing on national security, why would they care or waste their time?"

"It's like the argument that if you're not doing anything wrong, you have nothing to hide," she counters. "That may be true, but it's hardly the point. It's about the basic human right to privacy."

Visions of the young man drift through my mind. Why didn't he say they were *listening* to us through the phone? He said they were *watching*…

"It's not exactly easy to get a court order to listen in on someone's phone line. Believe me, it'd make my job a lot easier if we could monitor these people that way whenever the hell we wanted, but we can't. There are laws, Remy."

"You think these types care about laws?"

"What types?"

"Probably some shadow group hiding behind national security like they all do."

"Shadow group?"

Remy gives me a coy smile. "Too tin foil hat of me?"

"Little bit."

"Hey, you never know," she says with a wink, "you know?"

"Come on, you really believe we're under government surveillance?"

"Well, no. But it's not like it's never happened. Look what the Stasi accomplished back in the East Germany days. And that was years ago. With the technology available now…"

Don't use the house phone. They're watching you.

"This isn't East Germany."

"Doesn't matter, we're all human beings. Same flaws, same weaknesses, same susceptibility to corruption and abuse of power."

"That much is true anyway."

This time it's Remy who shrugs, her attention drawn back to the TV and the local weather report now being delivered by a perky blonde meteorologist in a skintight yellow dress. She reminds me of a giant misshapen lemon.

"Honey?" Remy asks suddenly.

I look to her. She appears concerned.

"Are you all right?"

"Yeah, I—I'm fine. Just a little tired is all."

She smiles and pats the section of couch next to her.

"Actually, sweetie, I'm going to skip the news this morning if you don't mind."

"Oh. Okay."

"Think I'll grab a shower a little earlier than normal. I've got a long day ahead of me at work today, and a backlog of paperwork to get done."

"You're not going to be late tonight, are you?"

"Don't plan to be, no."

"Good," she says, smiling again. "I'm making chicken stir-fry for dinner tonight."

"Sounds great," I tell her as I start for the stairs.

But she's already back under the spell of the television, and I've slipped under the waves surrounding me of late, waves that pull me down beneath the surface, where they surely intend to drown me.

As I ascend the stairs, I begin trying to convince myself that the strange man in the yard is nothing to worry about.

I fail. Miserably.

* * *

The lone window in the master bathroom overlooks our backyard. I stand there watching the fire pit and the chairs and the fence, as if expecting them to yield pertinent information that will help me understand what the hell took place out there earlier. The steam from the shower engulfs me, fogs up the mirror over the double sinks and fills the room with a ghostly mist. I want to hide in it, but there is false solace here, no means of escape. Like whispers in an empty house, echoes of unanswered prayers heard by no one, it hisses in my ears and reminds me how dangerous it is to balance one's life on the edge of a razor blade.

There's nothing you can do, Cam. There's nothing anyone can do.

I turn away from the window and back into the fog; watch my distorted reflection in the mirror. I look so old, so tired. Yes, that's it, *tired*—hopelessly, irreversibly tired—and it makes me think of the young man and the black bags beneath his eyes. His face comes to me, then fades away. But he remains, because he's never truly left.

Already nude, I open the shower stall door and step inside, into the hot water. It feels good on my tight muscles, pulsing against my stiff neck and down across my shoulder blades, so I give myself to it completely.

"What's happening to me?" I mutter the words, but the water running over my bowed head and across my open mouth even further slurs my speech. "Am I awake?"

I feel a sudden tightness in my chest, and wonder if I'm having a heart attack. Once a person hits forty these things become a concern. I tell myself it's likely gas or simply stress, as I'm experiencing none of the other symptoms everyone always says they have. No tingling sensation, no shortness of breath, no sweating, no shooting pain down my left arm, no jaw pain, just pressure on my chest, like someone's sitting on it with all their weight. Before I can think any more about it, I let out an enormous burp, the baritone sound bouncing along the shower walls and echoing all around me.

The pressure lessens, and by the time I've stepped out of the shower to dry off, it's gone completely. But as I reach for the towel on the bar a foot or so away, I see red smeared across the top of my hand. I raise both hands closer to my face. My knuckles are scraped raw and bloody and look as if I've been punching a cement wall.

Shocked and confused as to how I could've missed this prior, I go to the sink, turn on the hot water and reach for a bar of soap on the counter. My hand freezes above the soap dish, and then begins to tremble.

The scrapes and blood are gone. Frantically, I inspect my other hand. It's fine. But it's shaking now as well. I step back from the sink and drop down onto the toilet.

Sitting there on the closed lid and dripping on the floor, I stare at my hands and concentrate as hard as I can. A moment later, the shaking ceases.

The mirror is completely fogged over from the steam, but somewhere within all the blurry mess, I can see the vague outline of my body reflected back. Not quite me, but something similar...close...

And above my reflection, written with a finger in the condensation, is a perfectly legible sentence.

Something bad is going to happen.

CHAPTER TWO

After a thirty-minute commute to Boston, I park in a lot our department uses not far from South Station, then walk the remaining three blocks to my office. I force myself to admit that the writing on the mirror could only have been written by me. Apparently I'd forgotten doing it, didn't realize I had, or blocked it out somehow. There is no other reasonable explanation. I'm losing my grip on reality, and it's getting worse. That's the point. I feel like a thief slipping through the world trying to appear inconspicuous and undetected but all the while knowing it's only a matter of time before I get caught. And I know Remy is beginning to worry, she's becoming suspicious. She's noticing the signs, the changes in me, and I'll only be able to put her off for so long.

The morning air is brisk but not too cold yet, and the walk does me good, allows me time to pull myself together and ready myself for the day ahead. All that awaits me is eight hours of hanging on and pretending everything's fine when it's anything but, I know that all too well at this point, but there isn't a damn thing I can do about it.

When did this all start? I haven't always been like this, but I can't pinpoint a jumping-off point. It just...happened. No warning or known reason. Is that even possible? Do people simply lose it; just suddenly begin to slip away into madness?

I always used to wonder if insane people knew they were crazy. I suppose some have no idea whatsoever, but maybe that comes later. Maybe the actual process of losing one's mind is different. I can feel myself drifting away, things making less and less sense, and with every passing day I feel less like myself. That's worse, because it's like someone else is slowly taking over. He looks and sounds like me, but he's not me. He's someone else. Someone I don't know. And I can't stop him.

Briefcase in hand, I hurry across the street, dodging cars as I go, and move through the double front doors of my office building. After crossing a small lobby, I wait for the elevator with a couple other people who work in the building but not in my department. Though I recognize both, I don't know their names. We've never said a word to each other. Our interactions are always the same, slight nods of recognition followed by brief noncommittal smiles and then a silent ride to our floors.

My office is a satellite, a branch of the Office of Public Safety and Security, and is located on the sixth floor of a nondescript government building in the Back Bay section of the city. It's a small office (and one of a few others in the Commonwealth) that specializes in registering and tracking registered sex offenders. Our office houses six caseworkers (including myself) and our supervisor, Rosalind Calhoun. It's a relatively bare bones kind of office, but I always spend more time in the field than behind my desk anyway. It's a personal preference in how I do the job. It varies from employee to employee. Even though the procedures we must follow are written in stone and by law cannot ever vary, we still have our individual styles in terms of how we best implement those procedures and get the job done.

I haven't even reached my desk when Rosalind signals me into her office.

A cramped and cluttered area, her workspace is essentially a little glass cube positioned at the rear of the office. As Rosalind is notoriously disagreeable until she has her first few cups of coffee, being called into her office first thing in the morning is never a good sign. When she closes the door behind me, I know it's even worse.

"Morning," I say in what I hope is a pleasant tone. "What's up?"

"Have a seat," Rosalind says evenly, motioning to one of the chairs in front of her desk. "We need to talk a minute."

Without making eye contact, she moves around to her high-back leather swivel chair and, with a sigh, drops into it. In her mid-fifties, she's been working for various government agencies for over thirty years, and this one in particular for the last twenty. Divorced, she has two children and five grandchildren, and lives in nearby Revere with her boyfriend. Except for a four-year stint in the military, she's worked as a public servant for the Commonwealth in one capacity or another for her entire adult life. Although we've worked together the last twelve years, except for the occasional department-related function or Christmas party, we never socialize, so I really don't know her outside the office. As a boss, however, she is fair and effective and someone I've always gotten along with quite well professionally.

My hope is that her need to see me is related to some new case, improperly filed paperwork or something equally mundane. But when she still doesn't make eye contact, and instead snatches a pen from her desk and taps it repeatedly against her blotter, I know this is something more, as she only does this when she has something serious to discuss or is about to hand out a major ass-chewing. I sneak a quick peek over my shoulder. Although everyone else has arrived, no one looks in our direction.

"How're you doing, Cam?" Rosalind asks with an air of what

can only be caution.

"I'm fine."

"No. I mean it." Her dark eyes finally meet mine. "How are you?"

"Roz, I'm fine," I assure her. "Why?"

"The last week or so you…well…you haven't exactly been yourself." A trim, fit and orderly woman with a penchant for pantsuits and high heels, her black hair is styled in a super short Afro she's likely worn since her days in the military, although in the last few years it has become flecked with gray. Except for her power red lipstick, her makeup is hard to detect, if she wears it at all, and when I look at her, I am always drawn instantly to the intensity of her eyes. Both beautiful and somewhat intimidating when she wants them to be, they stare at me now with an unwavering sense of purpose. Cool, detached, all business. "You've been acting peculiarly. You seem distracted… *troubled*."

"I've had a heavy caseload lately, that's all."

"The budget cuts have made more work for all of us," she reminds me as she sits back in her swivel chair. "But that's not the issue here. Is everything all right at home?"

The question catches me off-guard. "At home?"

"Yes, at home. Is everything all right?"

"I don't understand. What's this all about?"

"Are you having problems at home, Cam?" she presses.

"Frankly, Roz, it's inappropriate for you to question me about my personal life." I offer a smile but can tell by the way it feels that it's likely coming off as stiff and forced. "But yes, everything's fine at home. What's going on? Have I done something wrong?"

"I'm concerned."

I feign confusion. "About what?"

"You," she answers. "Obviously I'm concerned about you. You've been at this job a long time and I've never seen you act like this before."

"Your concern is appreciated—sincerely—but what have I

done to warrant it?"

"Remember our talk last week?" Rosalind sits forward again and this time plants her forearms on her desk. "When I asked if you were feeling all right and you told me everything was fine, that you were just tired?"

A vague memory of this comes to me, a brief conversation in passing I hadn't given much thought to. "Yes, I remember."

"Well things have only gotten worse since then."

I want nothing more than to get out of her office and to be as far away from this conversation as I can get, but I'm trapped. At least for the time being, I have to stay even and do my best to come off like none of this is a big deal. "If I seemed distracted or—I'm sorry—what was the other word you used?"

After a beat she says, "Troubled."

"Right. Troubled. Okay. If I've seemed distracted or *troubled*, I apologize. I'm swamped with this current caseload and I've been working too hard, I guess. Maybe I'm overdue for a vacation, just need some rest and a break from all the..."

"Yeah," Roz says, sighing again. "Thing is, it's not just me. Your coworkers have noticed your behavior of late as well, and it's having an effect on the entire office. You've been mumbling to yourself and you act like you're somewhere else entirely. People ask you questions or try to talk with you and oftentimes you walk right past without even acknowledging them, and not because you're being rude, but because—at least this is how it appears, correct me if I'm wrong—you simply don't hear them or in some cases don't even realize they're there."

"Roz, I—"

"The other day Marianne said you were sitting at your desk staring into space with tears running down your face."

"That's ridiculous," I say, laughing lightly. "I did no such thing."

"Are you suggesting Marianne's lying?"

"No, but—I don't know, I—maybe she misinterpreted what she saw." As I fumble for more answers, I remember coming to in the office a few days before and wiping tears from my face. I thought I'd fallen asleep, but couldn't explain the tears, then or now. "The point is—"

"There's also been a complaint."

"Someone's made a complaint about me?" I ask, mystified.

She looks away, disgusted. "Yes, a registrant. Alfred Copeland."

My mind races and quickly locks on the name. A new registrant I visited a few days before. But I can't come up with any reason why he'd complain, I remember it going smoothly, a routine visit and registration. "Is it a *formal* complaint?"

"No. I spoke with Mr. Copeland's attorney on the telephone and—"

"He has an attorney? How'd he manage that so quickly and with no money?"

"Evidently, and I have no idea. Regardless, I apologized for your behavior and he didn't push the issue, but if what he told me is accurate, he had every right to, Cam. Whatever we think of these people, we still maintain a level of professionalism and—"

"Come on, Roz, seriously?" I place my briefcase on the floor next to me and fold my arms across my chest. "In the twelve years I've worked here, have you ever known me to behave unprofessionally?"

"No," she says.

"What was it I supposedly did?"

"He claims he allowed you into his apartment with no resistance and that you were in the process of welcoming him to the Commonwealth and going over the normal procedures when you suddenly became hostile." Roz shuffles through some papers on her desk until she finds a small notepad. After flipping through several pages, she apparently lands on the notes she took while speaking with Copeland. "He said you became very quiet, and he thought you might be having some sort of seizure as you wouldn't answer him and apparently became completely unresponsive. Then he says you suddenly snapped out of it and turned hostile, telling him he was evil and that the Devil was there in his apartment with the two of you. He said you told him you knew this because you could see the Devil watching him. Then you took your paperwork, angrily demanded he sign it and exited the premises." She tosses the pad aside. "Can't imagine why he'd want to complain about that, can you?"

"First of all, that's nonsense. I never said those things or behaved in that or anything even remotely close to that manner." I honestly didn't remember if I had or not, but I need to protect myself, and while I don't want to play this card, I do it anyway. "Secondly, this is a level-three offender who has done not one but two stretches in prison out-of-state for sexually assaulting girls under the age of thirteen. You're telling me you believe him over me?"

"Normally no, of course I wouldn't. But given your recent behavior here, I'd be remiss in my duties as the head of this office if I didn't take Copeland's complaint seriously. I managed to talk his attorney out of filing a formal complaint, so there's nothing in writing and there won't be any investigation or paper trail documenting this ever happened. You're welcome."

"Thank you," I reply reluctantly.

"Are you telling me Copeland made this all up?"

"Yeah, Roz, that's what I'm telling you."

She lets her pen rest in the corner of her mouth and watches me awhile. "Here's what I'd like to do," she says. "I'd like to put you on temporary leave—with pay—and I'd like you to submit to a full physical as well as a general psych evaluation."

"You can't be serious."

"Do I look like I'm anything but serious?"

"And if I refuse?"

"Well, then there's a chance this could get messy, because I can't keep ignoring your behavior. This is a sensitive job with sensitive responsibilities—you know that—I can't have loose cannons working in this office. I can't have it, Cam. Got me? I don't care how many years you have in or how good you are at your job." Rosalind calms a bit. "Whatever the problem is, let's figure out what it is now and get it handled and then we can all move forward. That work for you?"

It doesn't, but I don't have much choice, and we both know it. "When would this paid leave begin?" I ask.

"Immediately."

"I have some paperwork I'd like to finish up today and—"

"I've already assigned it to Sanchez, no worries."

"What about my new case?"

"Clark's going to handle it." Rosalind places her pen down on the blotter, delicately, as if she's afraid she might otherwise break it. "I can't have you in the field or even riding a desk until I'm certain you're fit for service. I'm sorry."

I nod, feel my face flush. "So how does this work from here then?"

"You can go on home. The department will be in touch regarding the general practitioner and psychiatrist they'll want you to see. Once the results are in, we'll take it from there."

"Okay then." I stand, grab my briefcase and try not to show any emotion.

"Cam," Rosalind says, standing as well. "I...I'm sure things will work out. You're a valuable asset to this office and have been for a long time. Your health and well-being is what's paramount here, I want you to understand that."

"I do understand. It's fine."

"Go home, get some rest."

Barely able to contain myself, I leave the office.

But I can't go home. Not yet.

* * *

Outside, I stand at the corner like a misplaced statue, traffic and people moving all around me like ghosts. I am alone in a city of hundreds of thousands. Cold and distant and so close I can reach out and brush it with my fingers, it's the same Boston I know so well, but also different somehow. Nothing seems quite right. Not here. Not anywhere.

"Cam!"

Accompanied by a sound reminiscent of horse hoofs striking pavement, Marianne Feeney hurries toward me with an awkward clopping gait, running in high heels as she hastily wrestles herself into a waist-length jacket. Twenty-seven, she possesses a head of thick shoulder-length red hair, striking emerald eyes and a pale, freckled complexion. From a family of hard-boiled Boston Irish cops, Marianne has only worked in the office for the last three years. Predominantly trained by me, she spent most of her first two weeks shadowing me while I showed her the ropes. Since then we've had a good working relationship, and she still comes to me from time to time for advice. Of all my coworkers, she's the only one I consider a friend. But when I left the office after my meeting with Rosalind, no one, including Marianne, looked at me or said anything.

"Hold on a minute," she says breathlessly, sidling up next to me. "Look, I want you to know that—"

"Don't worry about it, okay?"

"Roz called us all into the office one by one," she explains, snagging a renegade strand of hair with her fingers and hooking it behind her ear, "and asked us about your behavior because she'd seen it lately too. I didn't want to say anything but—"

"Marianne," I say firmly. "It's okay, relax."

"I just want you to know I wasn't throwing you under the bus."

"I don't think that, it's fine."

She frowns. "I'm worried about you, all right?"

"I know. Thanks, I—"

"That's why I told Roz what I'd seen."

"I understand."

She inelegantly adjusts the waistband on her skirt, then straightens her blouse. Regardless of what she wears, clothes always appear ill-fitting on Marianne, and she often seems uncomfortable in her own skin. "That day I found you crying at your desk you—Cam—you didn't even know who I was. You were sitting right in front of me, but you weren't there, not really. You were *gone*."

"I haven't been myself lately. I'm exhausted."

"You're sure there's nothing else going on? If you need to talk about it, I—"

"No. I appreciate it, but no. I just haven't been feeling well."

She watches me with her brilliant green eyes, weighing the validity of my response. I trained her well. Marianne knows bullshit when she hears it. "Remember what you told me when you were training me?" she asks, stepping aside so a group of people can pass and cross the street to the next corner. "You said this job can take a toll on us if we're not careful. The things we see and hear and deal with on a daily basis wear on us and can get into our heads. They get inside us, and they break us apart if we let them. That's what you said."

I smile at her fondly. "I remember."

"You've been working this gig a long-ass time. You need a break."

"They want me to get a physical and a psych eval."

"Are you going to do it?"

"Don't have any choice. Not if I want to keep my job."

"Then do it." She steps closer and places a hand on my shoulder. She smells fresh and clean, like a heady deodorant soap. "Get some rest and get away from this place awhile. Let the doctors do their thing. When you feel better, come back."

"What if I don't feel better?"

"None of us can do this job forever."

"I'm not in my twenties like you," I remind her sullenly. "Little long in the tooth to be starting over from scratch, wouldn't you say?"

"Come on." She rolls her eyes and flashes a bright smile. "You're only in your early forties. And besides, no job is worth your health and well-being. *No* job."

"That's good advice," I tell her. "Sounds familiar."

"I had a good teacher," she says with a wink.

I reach up and gently touch her wrist. "I've got to go."

"Yeah, I better get back up there. But if you need anything, don't hesitate, okay? I mean it. I'm around if you need me."

Her hand slips from my shoulder, and as I release her wrist, her hand slides into mine. I give it a squeeze. "Thanks, kid."

Marianne smiles and moves away, her hand pulling free as she's swallowed into a wave of people surging along the sidewalk like a single frantic organism. The last thing I see is that mane of red hair vanishing into the crowd. *Like fire*, I think. *Like fire...*

With the flames of a different fire—a distant and ancient fire, an unholy fire—inching closer, I turn and hurry across the street, disappearing into a crowd of my own.

* * *

Sometimes I take the train, but I drove to work that day, because I knew I'd be spending quite a bit of time in the field. A hard rain was falling, pouring from the heavens and soaking everything down. Rumbles of thunder growled in the distance, as if from some giant monster meandering across the city. Everything seemed slightly askew. Darker...a little colder...the city quiet beneath the steady deluge. I'd always found it strange and wondrous how rain often silenced the world, leaving only the sounds it made, its rhythms flowing like the breath of a greater, unseen consciousness.

Somewhere in all that rain, even before I'd reached my destination, I could sense some...other... something more there with me, whispering and laughing. But the words were gibberish, and the laughter had nothing to do with joy, only madness and wrath.

It was the laughter of demons.

I didn't believe in that sort of thing, and considered it nonsense that belonged in horror movies or scary novels, not the real world. Nonetheless, I was badly shaken, so I focused on the cadence of the windshield wipers, and it all eventually faded away, lost in the downpour. Yet something remained. There, with me, inside me, and I could do nothing but pretend it was all in my head—as if that somehow mattered—a dream, a fleeting thought I could escape simply by dismissing it.

I went directly to my first appointment, a new register I needed to take care of as soon as possible. In a less than desirable neighbor-hood in Dorchester, I found myself standing on the run-down porch of a duplex littered with bags of trash. In the far corner, an orange cat nibbled food from a plastic bowl. The animal glanced up at me with disinterest, then returned to its breakfast. I knocked on the front door.

I heard locks disengage and then the door slowly creaked open. A rotund man about my age stood before me in a pair of plaid flannel pajama bottoms and a tank top T-shirt. Bald but for sprigs of hair jutting out on either side of his head, he was unshaven and looked as if I'd wakened him. His eyes...there was always something in their eyes...something wrong...broken maybe. Some might call it evil.

"Alfred Copeland?" I asked.

The man looked beyond me at the street and then up to the sky, like he'd only then realized it was raining. "Yeah," he said in a gravelly voice.

"Cameron Horne, Office of Public Safety and Security."

After I showed him my ID, he stepped back and allowed me entrance. "Didn't think you'd be coming this early," he mumbled, straightening what little hair he had with his fingers. "I would've been, you know, ready."

"It's not a problem," I assured him. "This won't take too long."

Copeland's first-floor apartment was all but empty. No furni-ture, sheets tacked up over the windows. In the kitchen, an over-turned box of cereal lay on the counter next to a bowl of soured milk, and, as I placed my briefcase on another section of counter, I glimpsed an empty adjacent bedroom with a bare mattress lying on the floor. Two magazines and a roll of toilet paper were next to it. I glanced at Copeland. The look on his face told me all I needed to know. Over the years I'd come to know that look quite well. He was nervous and didn't want me there. But then, registrants never did.

"Just moved in," Copeland said with a smirk, like he saw some-thing familiar in me. Drifting over to the bedroom doorway, he casually pulled the door closed. "I start work tomorrow, so hope-fully I can get some furniture and basic stuff soon."

I'd read his file previously. A convicted pedophile and sexual sadist, Copeland had been incarcerated twice in his native Rhode Island for sexually assaulting young girls. None of his victims were more than thirteen years of age. Upon his release from prison, he'd moved to Massachusetts. "Where are you working?" I asked.

"Diner a couple blocks over. Washing dishes and busing tables."

"What brings you to the Commonwealth?"

Copeland scratched at his crotch. "Do I have to answer that?"

"I'm not a police officer, Mr. Copeland, I'm a public servant. My job is to get you registered with the Commonwealth and track you as a registered sex offender in our system. The more cooperative you are, the smoother this will go and the less chance there is other authorities will need to become involved, understand?"

"Sure, I get it." On the far side of the kitchen was a small bathroom, the door ajar. Copeland closed it as well. "I just wanted a fresh start, you know? Had my fill of Rhode Island, figured I'd give Mass a try."

"Are we alone here, Mr. Copeland?"

He smiled, his thin and badly chapped lips parting to reveal yellow and crooked teeth. "We're never alone if we walk with the Lord."

These types always claimed they'd found God in prison. The question was: Which god? I offered a quick and officious smile, then released the locks on my briefcase and flipped it open. "I mean, are we alone here in your apartment?"

"Sure, I live alone," he answered with that same creepy smile on his face. "But you already know that. You got the file on my whole life, right? There's no problem with me living in this place, is there?"

"Not so far," I told him. "It's an appropriate distance from any problem areas."

"Problem areas," he chuckled.

I gave him a look that made it clear I wasn't interested in exchanging small-talk or pleasantries. But he seemed unfazed and didn't look away. "Do you believe in the Lord, Mr. Horne?" he asked, his dark eyes disturbingly gleeful.

"I'm not here to discuss my personal beliefs." I located then removed the necessary forms from my briefcase. "We just need to do

some quick paperwork and then I'll go over a few things with you and be out of your way."

Thunder rolled as rain lashed the building, spraying the few dirty, uncovered windows, and further blurring the world outside. I watched the water sluice along the filthy panes. There was something mesmerizing about it, as if I'd never seen such a thing before. Suddenly everything felt like a dream. Slower...indistinct...distorted...and an odd whisper...

"I know you, Horne. I know you."

And then I could hear Copeland talking again, and although I knew he was only a few feet away, it sounded like his voice was coming from a great distance. His speech took on an odd, clipped tempo, but I could no longer make out what he was saying.

It sounded as if he'd begun to pray.

* * *

When I close my eyes, the memories recede and fade to shadow, replaced with a vision of a rickety old elevator. I've seen this elevator before, but can't remember where or when. The doors open and an operator dressed in a formal and dated uniform waits for me, his hand poised above the row of buttons. He has no face, only smooth skin, cracked and dry like a desert floor where his eyes and nose and mouth should be. Yet he turns his head to me, as if he can see. I know the moment I step inside and the door slides closed behind me, the cables will snap and the elevator will plummet, falling through the shaft and screeching like a wounded animal. And then it will disappear into the bottomless darkness below, the faint echo of my screams in its wake.

I open my eyes and find myself sitting alone on a bench in the Boston Common not far from the duck pond. After parting ways with Marianne, I remember walking the streets in a daze, along Boylston Street to St. James Avenue, past the Park Plaza and onto Stuart Street, and finally into Chinatown. After wandering Chinatown awhile I made my way to the Theater District and then back over to the public park. With no idea how long I've been sitting on the bench, I check my watch. It is late morning. I've killed a couple hours.

My thoughts shift to Remy. I dread having to tell her what's happened at work, but I can't very well keep it from her either. Since school is out at two, she's usually home well ahead of me, so rather than wander the city all day, I decide to walk back to my car, drive home and wait for her there.

As I stand and turn to leave, a group of young mothers walk by, pushing their babies in strollers and chatting amongst themselves. One of them, a stout woman with dark blonde hair, stares at me as if not quite certain what she's looking at. She holds my gaze for several seconds, then separates from the others and slowly approaches me. As she stares, I force a smile, unsure of what else to do, but she doesn't return it. Instead, she continues to gawk at me, baffled.

While still trying to figure out what I've done to warrant such a reaction, an old homeless man with a wild shock of white hair and a matching beard sits down on the far end of the bench and rummages through a wrinkled brown paper bag in his hands.

"Are you a sheep among wolves?" the woman suddenly asks. "Or are you a *wolf* among sheep?" She crouches and quickly adjusts the straps on the stroller holding her baby in place.

"I don't…understand…"

"Pardon?" She looks at me as if for the first time.

"Why did you ask me that?"

She smiles pleasantly. "I'm sorry, are you speaking to me?"

Now it's my turn to stare.

"I didn't say anything to you," she tells me. Her smile slowly fades, replaced with a troubled frown. She stands and hurries away.

Cackling laughter returns my attention to the homeless man. Filthy and wearing a long ratty coat, his feral, bloodshot eyes bore straight through me with an intensity somewhere between fear and desperation. His breath is sour and nauseating, and as he laughs even harder, his hair falls across his face. He leaves it there, one eye peeking out at me from behind the long, filthy strands. With a revolting squishing sound, something that resembles a huge slimy maggot pierces his eyeball, wiggling lose from the inside, and writhes its way free. It falls into the waiting bag in his lap. Still laughing, the man quickly rolls the top closed, his lone eye blinking and leaking blood and pus.

I pull my coat in tight around me and bolt for the street.

I do not look back.

* * *

The house is quiet. I'm not used to being home in the afternoon during the week, and that feels a bit strange, but regardless of the time of day or night, I've never been uncomfortable here before. Now I can't be so sure. I lock the doors and go up to our bedroom to change my clothes, but the minute I see the bathroom doorway I freeze. Heart racing, I force myself into the bathroom and look to the mirror. Nothing. Relieved, I run the water, splash a little on my face, then towel it off. I watch my reflection a moment. I want to believe it's me staring back—me and *only* me—and yet...

After slipping into some sweatpants and a sweatshirt, I collapse on the bed and lay there a moment, stare at the ceiling and try to calm myself. But I cannot ignore the feeling that I'm being watched. My head lolls to the side and I focus on the phone on the nightstand. I set it down on the floor, out of sight.

The world is coming apart all around me, slowly tearing at the seams. A strange young man in my backyard, bloody visions, words written on the bathroom mirror, lost memories and nightmares about Alfred Copeland, being put on leave from my job, the woman at the Common, the homeless man. It just goes on and on, water spiraling down a drain, pulling me deeper and deeper. I can't let it continue much longer. I know this. In my heart, I know it. Clearly the psych evaluation Roz is insisting on is for the best. But I'm frightened of what it might reveal. Or maybe I'm frightened because I already *know* what it will reveal.

My God, how did this happen? What's happening to me?

Maybe it's just exhaustion. The mind plays tricks when it's tired and run-down beyond a certain point. But not everything can be explained away so easily. These are either actual events or wildly lucid hallucinations and, unfortunately, both options are terrifying.

With a feeling of something lodged in the base of my throat, I lay still and tell myself it's only stress and anxiety. The tightness in my chest I experienced earlier that morning in the shower returns. *Breathe…breathe…*

My eyes roll shut. But I'm not asleep.

And I am not alone.

I bolt upright, gasping for breath, my eyes wide with terror. Did I fall asleep? The light is gone, replaced with shadows.

"Easy," Remy says. "Easy."

I turn toward the sound of her voice, see her lying there next to me on her stomach, watching me lovingly and rubbing my chest. My vision is slightly blurred, and I feel groggy and disoriented. "What's going on, I—did I fall asleep?"

She nods and smiles, strokes the hair on my chest with her fingers. "You were sleeping so soundly earlier I didn't want to disturb you."

"How long have I been asleep?"

"Not sure, you were asleep when I got home."

I reach back for my pillow, push it up closer to the headboard and prop myself up a little. "What time is it?"

"Almost ten, I was coming to bed myself."

"I've been asleep all day? How… How could that be?"

"You haven't been sleeping well lately," she says. "You must've really needed the rest."

I rub my eyes. My throat is dry and scratchy. "I'm still so… tired."

"Were you having a nightmare?"

My hand finds her face, and I gently rub her cheek to be certain she's really there and not some cruel dream. She's so beautiful. "I don't remember."

"Are you hungry? There's some leftover chicken stir-fry in the fridge."

"No, I—thanks—I'm sorry I missed dinner."

"Why were you home early?" She snuggles closer. "Did you come home sick?"

"Yeah, but—well, no—not exactly, I…" I wiggle free of her and sit up, swinging my legs around to the floor so I'm sitting on the edge of the bed, my back to her.

Remy reaches out and rubs my back. "What is it, sweetie?"

I push myself up to my feet and walk over to the window on shaky legs. Night has long since fallen, and except for a bright half-moon hanging in the sky, everything beyond my window is shrouded in darkness. "They put me on leave today," I tell her. "Paid leave, but still…"

"Why?"

I want to tell her everything, but can't. Remy needs me. She needs me to be strong and together and there for her, just like she's always been there for me. I don't even know how or where to begin. *They placed me on leave today because they're afraid I'm losing my mind. You know, like going bat-shit crazy. And oh, by the way, they kind of have a point because I'm pretty sure I* am *going bat-shit crazy; slipping into some sort of early dementia or senility—maybe it's even Alzheimer's—who knows? The point is my grip on reality is loosening and I'm afraid that if I admit it, even to you, somehow that will make it real, and therefore irreversible. And how was your day, sweetheart?*

"A registrant made a complaint against me," I explain. "He's lying, but by law the department has to follow up when something like this happens. They have to look into it, even if it's just going through the motions, which is all this is, and they have to put me on leave while the matter is investigated. It's a procedural thing."

Remy props herself up on her elbows, and the sparse moonlight through the window separates her into two halves, one light, one dark. "What was the complaint about?"

The Devil…do you believe in the Devil, Remy?

"A bunch of nonsense about me behaving unprofessionally."

"How long do you think it'll be before you can go back to work?"

"A week, maybe two, can't see it going any longer than that."

"Well, you're being paid the whole time," she says, rolling over onto her back and her side of the bed. "Take advantage of the time off. Get some rest and take it easy for a few days."

I stare down into the darkness surrounding the house. Nothing hidden, nothing moving or watching…it's just the night… and us.

"Come back to bed, sweetie," Remy says.

I close my eyes and a strange image darts through my mind: the sudden flapping of a bird's wings flying very close to my face. So close I can feel feathers brush my skin before it vanishes into the dark.

"Do you believe in the Devil?" I ask, opening my eyes and looking over at her.

"I believe in evil."

"*Literal* evil?"

"Is there some other kind?" she asks. "There's plenty of evil in the world, it's all around us. Look at the offenders you deal with. Aren't they evil?"

Countless faces and cases flood my memory and drift past my mind's eye, each one more disturbing than the last. "Most are sick or deeply troubled. Some would say they all are, and that evil's nothing more than an antiquated concept invented by ancient peoples unable to understand the psychology behind the darker side of human behavior."

"And do you agree with them?"

Do you believe in the Lord, Mr. Horne?

"No. I think some of them are evil."

"*Literally* evil?" Remy presses.

I nod.

"Well, then there you have it."

In the oddly quiet moment that follows, I almost feel like myself again.

Remy pats my side of the bed and smiles dreamily. I slip into her waiting arms, warmth radiating from her body like a pulse as she pulls me closer, tighter in against her, and peppers my face with soft little kisses.

"I love you, Rem," I whisper, holding her tight.

"I love you too," she whispers back.

And for just a little while, all the devils—imagined or actual—bow their heads, fold closed their leathery wings, and fall away to sleep.

CHAPTER THREE

I lie awake in darkness, listening to Remy's slow and steady breath. Asleep next to me, she moans softly, adjusts her position, then goes quiet. Mind racing and unable to sleep, I look over at the alarm clock. 3:33.

A strange sound distracts me. My eyes search the darkness and shadows until I lock in on the location it's emanating from: the closet on the wall to the left of our bed. But then it stops, so I listen a moment to make sure I'm right, and a few seconds later the sound returns. A soft but very definite sound of something scratching at the door; were it not the middle of the night and the house so deathly silent, I probably wouldn't have even noticed it. I sit up slowly, quietly, and stare at the closet door.

The scratching is coming from *inside* the closet.

We have no animals, and no one else is in the house…that I know of…so my guess is a rodent, perhaps a mouse. But it sounds bigger than a mouse…much bigger…

As the scratching ceases, I squint through the darkness and try to bring the closet into clearer focus. The small patch of moonlight breaking through the windows is the only illumination in the room, however, which makes visibility all but impossible. I can see a partial outline of the closet, and a small section of the door, but little else.

Quietly, I lean toward the floor and reach beneath the bed. After feeling around for a few seconds, I find the flashlight I keep there and pull it free. With a quick glance at Remy, I turn back to the closet, level the flashlight and switch it on.

Light punches a hole in the darkness, shines directly on the closet door.

The scratching resumes.

And then movement in the corner of my eye draws my attention to the right. I leave the flashlight trained on the closet door but peer toward the bathroom, where I'm certain the movement came from. It's too dark for me to make anything out, so I swing the flashlight 'round to illuminate the doorway, and just as the beam falls across the shadows, an enormous black mass separates from the darkness and darts out from the corner of the bathroom, scurrying toward me like an enormous spider. A man—or something like a man—rushes across the floor, its limbs clicking and crackling as it crab-walks on all-fours, bald, pale and pasty head spun impossibly backward, bulging demonic eyes glaring at me.

Screams of horror circle like a pack of ravenous wolves, the screeching growing louder and louder as in a mad scramble, kicking and flailing at the sheets and blankets until I'm free of them, I scramble back and against the headboard. Heart crashing in my chest, I extend an arm across Remy to protect her and frantically scan the floor.

Where is it? Where the hell is it?

But there's nothing there. Even the night has gone. Daylight fills the otherwise empty room. The spot Remy had occupied in bed is vacant, my arm hovering over an empty space. The alarm clock on the nightstand reads: 8:37. She's already at work.

Dreaming—Christ—I was only dreaming...

Yet the screams remain...distant but—no—not screams, that damn car alarm wailing in the distance.

Standing, I run my hands across my face and down along the back of my neck. Both are bathed in sweat. My body trembles.

God help me.

* * *

Downstairs, I find the coffee on and a note on the refrigerator from Remy telling me she loves me, and that Cliff called the night before and wants me to call him back. Cliff, my closest friend, is someone I normally see or at least talk to a few times a week. But I can't remember the last time I saw or spoke to him on the phone. He's left me voice mail messages for days, and I've returned none of them because I don't want him to know what's happening to me. I stare at the note a moment, and wonder if that's been a mistake. Maybe I should sit down and talk with him. Eventually I'll have to tell someone what's going on. Won't I? And when I do, it'll be the first time I've spoken to anyone about it. I'd rather it be Cliff than some shrink I don't know.

My hands are still shaking as I pour myself a cup of coffee.

The car alarm continues going off like it has every morning lately. But I rarely sleep this late. I'm up much earlier, so it usually goes off and wakes me hours before this. Is it coincidence that it's going off later today, on the very morning when I just so happened to sleep much longer than usual?

Coffee in hand, I wander over to the sliders and look out at the yard.

The young man is back, slumped in an Adirondack chair next to the fire pit.

Muttering, "Son of a bitch," I slam my mug on the kitchen counter, grab my cell phone, hurry to the sliders and yank them open. Not bothering with a coat, I step outside and cross the yard. The morning is chilly but sunny, the sky a bright, deep blue. The man is wearing the same outfit he had on before, a battered leather jacket, a sweatshirt, shabby jeans and worn boots. His dark hair is nearly to his shoulders, badly mussed and hasn't been washed in days, much less combed.

He raises his head, sees me coming, but doesn't seem to care.

"Who are you?" I demand while still several feet away.

"If you're not careful," he mumbles, "you'll kill him."

"What? Kill who?"

He digs a pack of cigarettes and a lighter from his jacket pocket with one hand, and brushes renegade strands of hair from his eyes with the other. "Everything's upside down." His face is riddled with torment and overwhelming frustration. "It's all in flames and wrong, it's—nothing's the way it's supposed to be."

"*Who* are you?"

He lights a cigarette, draws deep, then exhales through his nose, head bowed. "Everything you believe to be true…isn't."

"Why are you in my yard?" I step closer.

"Want me to come in the house instead?"

"I want you to answer the question."

"I told you before."

"Tell me again."

"I'm lost. I'm…waiting."

I shake my head. "No, you've come here purposely. Why? What do you want?"

He smokes his cigarette, says nothing.

"How do you know me?" I ask.

"I'm not sure I do. Or did…until recently."

I show him my cell. "Answer my questions or I'm calling the cops, understand?"

"It doesn't matter," he says. "It won't make any difference."

"Maybe I'll just physically throw you the hell off my property."

He offers a quick sideways glance in my direction. "Doubtful."

"You're in my yard," I remind him. "Uninvited. Again. *What* do you want?"

"I'm trying to help you."

"Then stop being cryptic and tell me who you are and what this is all about."

He nods, takes another drag on his cigarette. "Don't use the house phone."

"You said that last time."

"They're watching you through the phone."

"You said that too. What does that mean? Do you mean listening?"

"They're listening too."

"What about my cell?" I ask, holding it up again. "Is it safe or is it being monitored too?"

"Cell phones make it even easier for them to watch you."

"How does one watch someone through a telephone?"

"It's what they do."

"And who, exactly, are *they*?"

The young man stares into space as a single tear slowly rolls down the length of his cheek. In a loud whisper, he says, "You don't want to know."

Frustrated and upset as I am, I pity him. He appears to be exhausted and thoroughly destroyed emotionally, and for reasons I cannot yet understand, part of me believes he not only means me no harm, but that he may, in fact, truly be trying to help me. "Look, I—I don't know what's happening to me, okay?" My voice breaks, and I quickly clear my throat in an attempt to keep my emotions in check. "I think I'm losing my mind. I…I'm not sure what's real and what isn't anymore. I'm not even…" I draw a deep breath, let it out slowly. "I'm not even sure you're real or this conversation is actually happening."

He looks at me, such sorrow in his eyes. "Are you frightened?"

I nod.

A second tear spills free. "Me too."

Suddenly my cell rings, startling me. The young man nods, smirks and looks away, as if he'd known all along it was coming. I read the ID scrawled across the screen.

SHELLY HORNE.

"Christ," I mutter. My ex-wife Shelly is the last thing I need right now.

I let it go to voice mail.

Divorced for seven years, Shelly has never reverted to her maiden name, and unlike me, hasn't remarried. Though it's been months since I've heard from her, she periodically contacts me (even though I've repeatedly asked her not to), and has done so since we first split up. Every time she calls she's in trouble or drunk or both, and while I feel badly for her, and a part of me will always love her, it is precisely this kind of behavior that led to our divorce.

I haven't even returned the phone to my pocket when it rings again. She's calling back, and I know from past experience that if I don't eventually answer, she'll continue calling and leaving messages until I do. Again, I let it go to voice mail.

"When she calls back," the young man says softly, "answer it."

Before I can respond, Shelly calls a third time. This time, I answer. "Shell, listen, I can't talk right now, I—"

"Cam is—is that you?" her voice crackles.

"You called me, Shell, who else would it be? I can't talk now, I'm hanging up."

"Please." She breathes heavily into the phone like she's crying, or trying very hard not to. "Please, Cam…don't, okay? Just…don't."

"What's wrong?"

"I need you to…I need you—just listen, I—Cam, I…"

I can tell from the slur she's drunk. "I can't do this right now."

"Don't be mean to me, I…" Talking just above a whisper, she gasps, "*Please.*"

"What's the problem this time?"

A pause, and then: "I know what you did."

Something stirs deep inside me, like something asleep has suddenly come awake. I turn away, take a few steps from the young man and lower my voice. "What the hell are you talking about?"

Crying harder, she says, "I know a lot of stuff, I—I'm not stupid, you know!"

"Shelly, I'm in the middle of something. I don't have time for this."

"You—please—you've got to come get me, okay? I can't—I need you!"

"Christ. Are you serious?"

"I can't drive."

"Get a cab."

"I'm out of money, I..."

"Where are you?" I ask through clenched teeth.

"In a bar..."

Of course you are. I glance at my watch. "It's not even ten o'clock in the morning."

"I been up a...awhile."

Code for she's been bar-hopping all night. "Are you by yourself?"

"Uh-huh."

"Which bar this time?"

She says something indecipherable and then, "In Everett."

That information does not come as a surprise, since that's where she lives. "If you want me to come get you, I need to know where you are. Try to focus and listen to what I'm saying. What bar are you in right now?"

"Dirty E's," she sobs. "Hurry okay, I don't—I don't feel so good."

"Stay put. I'll be there soon as I can."

"Thanks, baby, I—"

I disconnect the call and turn back to the young man.

He's gone.

* * *

The city of Everett lies four miles north of Boston, so depending on traffic, it's about a thirty-five to forty-minute drive from my house. I've spent some time in Everett due to work, but I'm not all that familiar with it. Known for its highly successful high school football program, Everett has a diverse population and cross-section of neighborhoods, and while the majority of residents are honest, hardworking, law-abiding folk, Everett is also infamous for hardcore drugs and a relatively high crime rate. I'd been to Shelly's apartment a few times to drop her off after rescuing her from assorted bars in the area, so I knew how to get in, get there and get out, but that's about it. I let my GPS take charge, as it offers the fastest and allegedly easiest route to Dirty E's, no doubt a wonderful and wholesome establishment suitable for the entire family. I follow its instructions, but all I can think about is the strange young man's vanishing act.

I spun like a top in a frantic pirouette, searching for him but finding no trace. It didn't seem like there was enough time for him to get up and leave the yard, but evidently he did just that, as he was nowhere in sight. At first I dropped to my knees, certain I'd slid into a complete breakdown. Had I imagined the entire thing? Could that be possible? Was I *that* far gone? Then just as I was certain I'd crumble to pieces, I saw the cigarettes next to the fire pit. Flattened and mangled—mostly just filters—they lay in a haphazard pile in the grass right where he'd dropped and stepped on them. I crawled closer, scooped them up and squeezed my hands into fists, crushing the cigarette butts between my fingers. They were real. More than see them, I could feel, touch and smell them. And if they were real, then so was he.

The GPS unit leads me into Everett, and I pay closer attention as the directions become more complicated. Although it's a myth that all sex offenders run around in long raincoats and live in slums—most don't—there are times, because of my job, that I do find myself in bad areas, and often disturbing, potentially sticky situations. I know enough to focus on my surroundings and the task at hand, so I shake off the fear and confusion coursing through me as best I can. As the neighborhoods grow worse, I turn a corner and roll down what at first appears to be a deserted street. Several boarded-up and abandoned duplexes line the street, followed by an empty lot where a building has evidently been demolished not too long before, the area covered with bricks and debris. There is no one on this street. Maybe it's too early. Maybe everyone's left.

At the top of the block, my GPS instructs me to take a right.

I do, and turn onto a more commercially zoned street. Although several buildings are empty and all of them are dilapidated and in serious need of renovations, about halfway up the block I see the sign for Dirty E's hanging above a badly scarred metal door painted black. There is only one window, and it faces the street. A neon Budweiser sign blinks on and off behind the filthy pane. The bar is sandwiched between a ramshackle pawnshop and a horribly run-down strip club, both of which appear to be closed at the moment. I pull over and park across the street, making sure I get a spot with no one in front of me. I've learned from past experiences that sometimes you have to get out of and away from places like this quickly. I sit there a moment and watch the street. There is a small amount of traffic but hardly anyone on foot. Again, I focus on the task at hand, which is going inside and getting Shelly out of there with as little fanfare as possible. Everything else gets left outside that door, because I can already tell that this is the sort of place you don't go into weak or distracted. You present or carry yourself in the wrong way, it could get you killed.

My job has afforded me a certain degree of expertise in terms of dealing with people—particularly the underbelly of society and those who don't want to be dealt with—and although I can handle myself reasonably well in a scrap if need be, I've mastered controlling situations and people when necessary, and generally have strong enough communication skills to avoid physical confrontation.

Before I left home, I changed into casual clothes—jeans, sneakers, a pullover and a brown suede jacket—but brought my work ID with me, which I keep in a small leather case. I slide it into my back pocket, kill the ignition and hop out of the car.

As I cross the street, a strong industrial smell hangs in the air, mixed with other foul odors, and although the sun is still shining and the morning seems to be developing into a nice day, there is a sense of darkness here, of oppression and sadness so strong it's palpable. With a final quick look back at the street, I pull open the black metal door and slip inside Dirty E's.

Significantly darker here than on the street, it takes a few seconds for my eyes to adjust, but once they do, I see one long rectangle of a room that reminds me of a train car. But for a few tables against the back wall, the entire place is one big, badly worn wooden bar. The floors are an aged and cracked tile, badly stained and in desperate need of a good scrubbing, and the ceiling is low and dark, the walls covered with cheaply framed photographs of various New England sports teams. A silent jukebox sits in the corner, and a formless smell of body odor and old booze hangs in the air.

I quickly scan the room.

A burly middle-aged man with a boxer's nose, a gray buzz cut and a beer belly stands behind the bar. He raises a bushy, salt-and-pepper eyebrow, folds thick, heavily tattooed arms across his barrel chest and glares at me like I've just exposed myself. Three patrons occupy stools across from him: Shelly, bookended by two men. All three turn and look at me in unison. Shelly recognizes me immediately and offers a drunken grin, raising her glass to me in mock salute. One of the men, a heavyset thirty-something with balding but long, stringy hair, has his arm around her, and smiles at me with contempt. The second, a lean but muscular man wearing a bandana that sports the Brazilian flag, glances at me with disinterest before quickly returning to his beer.

"Hey!" Shelly says, waving with her free hand. "Come have a drink with us!"

As I cross the room, I toss the bartender a brief sideways glance, but my focus remains primarily on the man with his arm around Shelly. I offer him a quick nod of recognition.

The man tightens his grip on my ex-wife, pulls her closer and whispers in her ear. They both begin to laugh.

"You still need that ride, Shell?" I ask flatly.

"She's gonna get a ride," the man says, "but not from you, chief."

The bartender and the Brazilian both laugh, and Shelly joins in, though she's so drunk I'm relatively sure she has no idea what he said.

"You gonna be in here," the bartender says in a gruff voice, "you got to order something."

"It's ten forty-five in the morning," I remind him.

The look on his grizzled face assures me he could not possibly care less.

"Fine, give me a Coke."

The bartender rolls his eyes, then lumbers away as I turn back to Shelly and her two friends. "Let's go, Shell."

"Sit down and drink your Coke, Skippy," the guy with his arm around her says. "She's with me. Don't worry about it."

I work my head back and forth in an attempt to loosen the tension in my neck a bit. He's not as drunk as Shelly is, but I can tell he's had several. With a sigh, I take a slow look around. "I'm not worried about it," I tell him. "But you should be."

"You believe this fucking guy?" he asks the bartender. "Lace-curtain motherfucker coming in here like he's got a cock down to his frickin' knees."

The bartender slaps my Coke down in front of me and growls out an overinflated price. I pay him and he returns to the far end of the bar where he pretends to watch the blurry newscast playing on a television suspended in the corner.

I remain standing as I sip my drink. It's cool and feels good going down. "Okay, here's what's going to happen," I say to the man with his arm around her. "You're going to take your hands off her, and Shelly's going to get down off that stool and come with me. Then we're walking out that door and that'll be that. Got it?"

"Fuck off." He jerks a thumb at the door.

"Shelly, let's go," I say.

The man removes his arm from her back and spins round on his stool until he's facing me. His face is pasty, pale, and riddled with acne scars. "Why you being such a pain in my ass, guy? Who is she to you?"

Shelly leans into him, giggles, and in a theatrical whisper says, "That's my husband."

"Ex-husband," I correct her.

"Then what do you give a shit?" he asks.

I place my Coke back on the bar and reach for Shelly's arm. "Come on."

"Hey," the man snaps, grabbing hold of my wrist with a powerful grip.

I yank my arm free and square my stance.

"Look, I just met this slam pig," he says. "Bought her some drinks and we're having a good time. So screw."

I pull out my ID and hold it up to his face. "I'm with the Office of Public Safety and Security."

He squints at it with drunken confusion. "The fuck is that?"

The Brazilian guy eyes my ID, chuckles, then mumbles something in Portuguese.

"What are you, some sort of cop?" the man asks. "I don't see no badge."

"We track and register sex offenders in the Commonwealth," I explain. "What's your name?"

"Huh?"

"Your name, what is it?"

"Go suck a bag of dicks."

"What is that, Scottish?"

"I don't have to tell you shit."

"Bet you've got a rap sheet a mile long, don't you?"

"So what if I do? Not like I diddle kids. I ain't no pedo."

"You're about to be."

"Fuck's that mean?" He turns to the guy in the Brazil bandana. "Fuck's he talking about?"

Shelly sips her drink and giggles again.

"What it means," I say, "is that I'm ten seconds away from calling the cops and telling them you're a registered sexual predator who recently changed residences and didn't update his information. My office has been trying to locate you for months. Since you've been ducking us and you're a violent levelthree habitual offender, and therefore extremely dangerous, they'll lock your ass up until we get this all sorted out."

The man eyes the other two men. "Sounds like he's from the

People's Republic, don't he? What are you, one of them Cambridge homos?" He turns back around to the bar. "Don't worry, professor, I'll make sure your ex gets home."

Shelly frowns, slides down off the stool and stumbles a bit, falling back against the bar. "I don't..."

She lets out an enormous burp. "I don't feel good."

"Get that bitch out of here if she's gonna hurl," the bartender barks.

The Brazilian finishes his beer and nonchalantly signals the bartender for a refill.

"Shelly," I say, reaching for her, "now."

"Ain't telling you again," the man says, moving between us. "She's fine right where she is."

I pivot and fire an elbow up into his face. It lands with a sickening sound, square on his temple and with such force my forearm and fingers go numb almost immediately. He staggers away, then slowly drops to one knee, both hands pressed flat against his temple.

The bartender shouts something unintelligible and pulls a nightstick from beneath the bar, but remains where he is.

I grab Shelly by the wrist and pull her away from the bar, bringing her around behind me. I know I should leave. I should take Shelly and go—and I easily could—but for some reason, I don't.

The balding guy remains on one knee, grimacing and wincing and clearly so dazed he isn't quite sure where he is or what's happened.

I look to the Brazilian. He smiles at me. It's a creepy, knowing sort of smile. He places his thumb against his neck and runs it across his throat, as if slitting it.

Keeping Shelly behind me and the bartender in my line of sight, in two quick strides I reach the other man and throw a punch directly into his face.

In a spray of blood, snot and saliva, he falls back and lies there, nose shattered and gushing, running across his cheeks and chin and onto the floor. I stand over him, studying him a moment, but

I no longer feel like myself. It feels as if I'm on the other side of the bar watching this all go down.

Straddling him, I grab the front of his shirt and hoist him up off the floor about a foot or so. Limp and barely conscious, his eyes roll about in his head as I cock back my fist and slam it into his face. His head snaps back and he vomits, most of it running over his chin and onto my arm along with the blood. In my mind, I tell myself to drop him and move away. Instead, I hit him again. And again. Then I switch hands and pummel him some more.

Eventually, Shelly grabs me and begs me to stop.

"That's enough!" the bartender says, though he sounds impossibly far away.

I let the man go, leaving him beaten to a pulp and lying in a pool of his own blood and vomit. My shirt is sprayed with his blood, as are my neck and face. I can feel the warmth and stickiness congealing on my skin. With Shelly hanging on my arm, I stumble away from him and my eye catches the Brazilian, but he faces front and sips a fresh beer, minding his own business.

"Jesus!" The bartender hurries out from behind the bar. "You trying to kill him?"

I don't answer, because I'm certain the answer is yes.

If you're not careful, you'll kill him.

The strange young man's words and sad face come to me from the shadows. How could he have known about this before it happened?

"Take that skank and get the hell out of here," the bartender says, nightstick at the ready. "Don't come back, and make sure that alky cock-tease stays gone too, you hear me?"

I do, but by then Shelly and I are already heading out the door.

CHAPTER FOUR

The water feels cold against my flushed skin but does little to combat the feverish temperature surging through me. From the moment we arrived at Shelly's building, a two-story walk-up located in a better but still fairly rough neighborhood six blocks from the bar, it's felt as though I have a bad fever. I help her into her apartment, and then, sweating and light-headed, escape into the bathroom to pull myself together. Thoughts of the beating I gave the man in the bar refuse to leave me, replaying over and over again in my mind. The sounds. The feel. The blood. In retrospect, I am repulsed by my actions. But at the time the violence and brutality felt good. It felt right.

I push my hands back beneath the faucet and watch the steady flow of gray water accumulate in my cupped palms. I splash it on my face a second time, then grab a ratty hand towel from a nearby rack and force my eyes to the dirty mirror above the sink. Images disturbing yet familiar stare back—pale skin, disheveled hair, cracked lips and glassy eyes ringed with dark circles and saddled with puffy black bags—all mere consequences, perhaps distractions, from the unbridled terror and confusion that's stalked me for weeks now. "It'll be all right," I tell the reflection quietly. "Just hold it together, it…it'll be all right."

I wipe my face and hands, toss the towel aside and turn off the water. In the mirror, I see that the tops of my hands are red. I raise both hands closer to my face. My knuckles are scraped raw just as they'd appeared to be that morning before my shower. *Am I seeing the future? Is someone…something…showing it to me?*

Exiting the bathroom, I step directly into a dimly lit kitchen. Leaning against the counter, I scan the area as well as the small living room beyond. A wide shaft of sunlight powering through the kitchen windows creates shadows on either side of it, and except for the steady hum of the refrigerator, the apartment is quiet. When we were together, Shelly was always neat and clean, but even that has changed. Like the bathroom, nothing in the rest of her place has been cleaned or even straightened in ages. It looks as if no one has actually lived here in years. And maybe that's not so far from reality. Shelly's alive, but one would be hard-pressed to define her existence as anything that even approaches living.

Everything's upside down. It's all in flames and wrong.

Apollo, Shelly's cat, meows and jumps up on the kitchen counter. As he slinks over to me, I feel myself smile and reach out to pet him. "Hey, buddy."

Nearly twelve years old, Apollo was with us when Shelly and I were married. I still remember the day she brought him home from the shelter. *I looked into his eyes and it was like he knew the future,* Shelly said. *He knew I'd come for him, and that he was meant to be with us. I'm going to name him Apollo, after the Greek and Roman god of prophecy.* He was five when we divorced.

As Apollo begins to purr, I run my hand along his head and across his back, which he arches as he leans into me, giving me his feline version of a hug. It is then that I realize how skinny he's gotten. Often with advanced age, cats become quite thin, but I can feel every vertebrae in his spine, little knucklelike bulges against my fingertips. "For Christ's sake," I sigh, "when's the last time she fed you?"

After a quick search, I find two small plastic bowls on the floor next to the stove. Both are empty. I fill one with water from the kitchen sink, set it down, then scour the cupboards until I find a bag of dry cat food. It seems to be okay, so I pour some into the second bowl. Before I've finished, Apollo hops from the counter and enthusiastically begins to eat.

There's something profoundly beautiful about that. Sad, but beautiful, and for the briefest moment, while I watch him eat and remember how much I miss him, I feel connected to something greater than myself. Something benevolent and kind that watches over us both. I think of the young man in my yard, the pain in his eyes and the tears rolling down his face, and I want to cry too.

And then it's all gone and we're alone again, Apollo and I.

Like everyone else in this life, we're on our own.

In a hall closet, I find Apollo's litter box. It is overflowing with waste and smells horribly. After dumping it into the trash in the kitchen, I wash it in the kitchen sink, then refill and return it to the closet.

Moving down the short hallway into Shelly's bedroom, I step over the clothes strewn along the floor and draped over the furniture and stand next to the bed where I left her. I expect to find her asleep or unconscious, but she's awake, her sad blue eyes looking up at me through a haze of drugs and alcohol.

"Hey, baby," she says pensively.

Somewhere deep inside her, I can still see the woman I once loved. But she's dying, a flame slowly flickering toward extinction. I pull her leather boots off, drop them on the floor with the rest of the mess, then sit next to her on the side of the bed. Her short blonde hair is mussed, her makeup smudged and her clothes wrinkled and worn.

"I'm going to take Apollo," I tell her.

Her expression goes from dreamy to confusion, then anger. "No, you're not."

"He hasn't eaten in days. You can't care for him anymore."

"Yes, I can, I—I was just gone for a little while and forgot to put food down."

"How long have you been partying?"

Her head lolls to the side, cheek against the dingy pillow. "Couple days, I think."

"Apollo's an old man," I remind her. "Do you want him to die?"

Her lips slowly curl into a devilish grin. "Apollo can never die."

"It's not a joke, it's abusive. I'll take him and give him a good home with us."

"You're not taking my fucking cat," she snarls. "He's all I have left!"

She tries to sit up, to scratch at me with her hands, but is too weak and fails. I catch her wrists and pin them down by her sides, pushing her deeper into the mattress and holding her there a moment. "Stop it." She continues to struggle, so I move my hands to her shoulders and give her two strong shakes. "Shell, stop!"

Shelly goes limp, smiling and laughing quietly. "You want to hit me, Zeke?"

Zeke?

"Jesus Christ." I let her go. "Do you even know who I am?"

"Do *you* know who you are?"

"You just called me Zeke."

"Did I? I'm wasted, I…" Her eyes roll around as if she's lost control of them, then she squirms around a bit and reaches for me again, this time more tenderly. Her hands find my arm and her fingers glide slowly up and down, from my elbow to my wrist, then back again. "Come home, baby. Please come home to me. It's where you belong."

"You've got to move on, Shell. We're over, and we have been for years."

"You think your perfect little life with your perfect little job and your perfect little wife is gonna save you?" She chuckles, but it's a mean and scornful laugh.

"My life and job are hardly perfect."

"Oh, but that little cunt you're with is, huh?"

"Don't call her that. You don't even know her."

"Fuck her. You belong with me and Apollo. Come home, Cam. Come *home*."

"This isn't my home. We never lived here together."

Shelly narrows her eyes, as if she's losing sight of me. "Where did we live?"

Much as I despise the way she lives her life, I can't help but feel sorry for her as well. She's a mess, and while I'm not to blame for her problems, if I'm honest, I can't completely excuse myself—or perhaps my absence—from being a partial contributor to her collapse. But even when we were together, Shelly was hardly a pillar of stability. She was always a train wreck. It's just a matter of degrees. Maybe I thought I could save her. Maybe I thought doing so might save me. It doesn't much seem to matter anymore either way. I put my hand on her forehead and gently run it back into her hair. Despite the chill in the apartment, she's covered in perspiration and her skin is clammy and pale, unhealthy-looking. "You should try to get some rest, okay?"

"I don't look so good anymore, do I?" she asks.

"You'll be fine, just sleep."

"The drugs and the booze, they…they catch you after a while, you know? They catch the best of us, baby."

"That's why you need to rest."

"You used to think I was so sexy." A smile crosses her face like a spasm. There, then gone. "You used to say I was the sexiest woman you'd ever seen. Remember? Remember when you used to say that, baby?"

"Yes," I answer softly, although my memories of our life together are vague at best. Much of it was so unpleasant that I've blocked most of it out. "I do."

"You used to like me. You used to love your naughty girl."

"It's a different life now."

Her glazed eyes lock on mine. "Are you sure about that?"

"You can't keep doing this. You need to get some help, Shell. Rehab or…"

"We had so much fun. Didn't we?"

"Sure."

Her fingers tighten on my arm. "You don't look so good either, you know. And you're burning up, I—I can feel it on your skin. See? We're no good without each other. Come home."

"Go to sleep," I tell her. "You'll feel better if you just go to sleep."

She watches me awhile. She knows me too well. "You're losing it too, aren't you? Right down the goddamn rabbit hole with the rest of us, huh?"

"What do you mean?"

"Fuck you think I mean?" she asks dreamily, her speech still slurred.

At this point Shelly is the last person I want to confide in, yet something feels right about doing just that. Familiarity, perhaps, as there's a certain unspoken comfort in it, and if nothing else, we still have that between us. Problem is, in her condition, how can I trust anything she says? I risk it anyway. What do I have to lose?

"Do you know what's going on?" I ask.

"Don't you?"

I shake my head no.

"It's all gone to shit, baby. Square pegs don't fit in round holes, no matter how hard you try to force it. You belong with me."

In a loud whisper I tell her, "I feel like I'm losing my mind, Shell."

"You think I'm the only one who knows what you did?"

"You said before you knew what I did. What are you talking about?"

Somewhere in the distance, a siren sounds, then fades.

"What have I done, Shell?" I press. "What have I done?"

"You ran away. You ran away and left me."

"Part of me will always love you, but our life wasn't what I wanted. I'm sorry."

"You think that matters?" she asks, her anger replaced with sorrow.

I don't answer. There seems little point. We're going around in circles. She doesn't know anything more than I do. She's a drunk and a drug addict, nothing more, nothing less.

She bends her leg at the knee and rubs her bare foot against my side. "Lay down with me awhile."

"I can't."

"We'll just snuggle, I promise." Her hands move up and onto my chest. "Come on," she whispers. "Come *on*. You know you want to. You can do anything you want to me, baby. *Anything…*"

I remove her hands as gently as I can, place them back down at her sides. "I got to go. If I find Apollo in this kind of shape again, I'm taking him, you understand?"

"Take him," she says, tears filling her eyes. She rolls over, away from me, and tangles herself in a sheet. "Take him home to your perfect little bullshit life. I'm sure Little Miss Fucking Awesome can take better care of him than I will. You took everything else from me, why not Apollo too?"

Just then, as if on cue, the cat hops up onto the bed and lies down against Shelly's back. I reach down and give him a pat on the head as he settles in for a nap. "I mean it," I tell her. "If I find him like this again, he comes home with me."

She lies there with her back to me, says nothing.

"I have to go." I reach for her, my hand hovering in midair over her shoulder. "I'll call tomorrow and check in on you, okay?"

"No, you won't."

I slowly return my hand to my side.

After a moment, Shelly's breathing grows heavy and steady. She's drifted off to sleep. I grab the sheet to pull it free of her lower body and cover her properly, but something moves beneath the covers near her leg, tenting the sheet as it slowly slithers toward her waist.

I jump back, horrified but unable to take my eyes from the bed as the long, thick bulge glides beneath the sheet, slowly coiling around her with a sickening wet sound.

Something white and slimy, much like the giant slug from the homeless man's eye, reaches the very edge of the sheet, twisting slowly back and forth as if searching for purchase.

I slam shut my eyes, tell myself this is not happening. It is not happening because it is not possible. It is not real, goddamn it. *It is not real.*

When I open my eyes, all I find is Apollo staring at me quizzically.

Shelly is fast asleep. There is nothing else there or moving beneath the sheet.

Are we alone here, Mr. Copeland?

Shaken, I leave the apartment. Once outside, as I hurry down the steps to my car, I realize something else is wrong. At the base of the front stairs, I look to the sky. It has turned a dull gray, and the sunshine from earlier has vanished, replaced with a bank of thick, dark clouds. I look at my watch: 3:33 PM. Half the day is gone, and it's taken the sunshine with it. Night is coming, and this time of year it will arrive within the next hour or so.

But how is this possible? It should still be late morning—early afternoon at the latest. How long was I in Shelly's apartment? It seemed like a short while, perhaps half an hour. But if my watch is correct, I've been in that apartment for hours. What the hell was I doing in there?

A strange darkness deep within me comes loose just then, crashing over me like a rogue wave. Horrible bursts of unspeakable carnage blink in strobe light flashes across my mind's eye, and terrifying screams of agony ring in my ears.

I have never been a religious man, but I know what I'm seeing and hearing.

The flames spread closer.

* * *

Rocketing through the dingy streets of Everett, I make my way toward the highway, hoping to leave at least some of these nightmares behind me. My mind races, filled with visions and voices, confusion and terror. Despite the car heater, I am freezing and sweating all at once. Suddenly ravenous, I pull over at the first eatery I see, a little hole-in-the-wall place advertising an array of greasy specials.

A little bell jingles over the door as I enter, and I am greeted by the smell of fried food, an empty dining area and the disinterested glance of a teenage girl working the counter. I stand before the counter, looking up at the massive menu board suspended overhead.

"Welcome to Rickey's," the girl sighs in monotone, "how may I take your order?"

"Let me get a double cheeseburger," I tell her. "Rare."

I usually like meat cooked medium, but for some reason I want it bloody and hot and running right now. I can almost feel the warm blood smearing my lips and dripping down my throat.

"Make it two double cheeseburgers, very rare, make—make sure they're really rare, okay? And I'll take a hot dog too—no—a chili dog with onions and cheese. And fries, I—a large fry and—do you have milkshakes?"

"Yeah," she says, as if answering requires enormous effort on her part.

"I'll have a chocolate one then, please. The biggest one you've got."

"That's to go?"

"I'll eat it here."

Her eyes widen, clearly surprised that all the food is for me, but she rings me up, hands a cook at a grill behind her the ticket, then turns back to take my money.

I'm shaking and starving and light-headed, but manage to pay her, then find a seat at the closest table and wait. My mind continues to scream, my leg bouncing up and down like a nervous school kid. I'm freezing, but covered in sweat. My fever must be getting worse. Starve a cold, feed a fever. Isn't that what they say? Or is it the other way around? I don't care, I need food and I need it now.

What seems an eternity passes before the girl brings my order on a large plastic tray, places it before me without a word, then returns to her position behind the counter, where she stares at me as if to be certain I'm really going to eat all this.

I attack the tray like a wild dog, stuffing a burger into my mouth and chewing noisily, slurping milkshake and scooping up handfuls of fries at a time. I know what I'm doing, in that I understand and am aware of my actions, but I don't feel as though I'm in control of them. I never eat or behave this way, but it's as if I've become a marionette controlled by some unseen puppeteer, and although I know damn well I'm making a spectacle of myself, I can't stop.

Within a few quick moments, the food is gone and I'm finally sated.

I sit there a moment like a blob, feeling like I've just eaten a family of four, my stomach gurgling and my chest tight. The sweats grow worse, so I down the rest of the milk shake, hoping it will cool me, and it does, but only temporarily. When I look up from my meal, I see that the cook has joined the girl at the counter. Both stare at me like they've never seen anything quite like what they just witnessed.

"You all right, buddy?" the cook asks.

"Yeah," I lie, forcing myself up out of the chair.

He points to a silver holder on my table. "There's napkins right there."

I grab a handful, wipe my mouth and chin clean, thank him under my breath, then hurry back out to my car.

Three blocks later, I pull over, stumble from the car and vomit into the gutter.

* * *

By the time I arrive at home and park in our driveway, dusk is in full bloom and the sky has morphed into a peculiar shade of gray. Could be threatening rain, perhaps even an early snow—can't be sure—but it's gotten noticeably colder. I sit in the car a moment, watch the house. Such a nice little Colonial, well maintained, the soft glow of lights in the windows warm and inviting. And inside waits Remy, the woman of my dreams, probably worried about where I am and seconds away from texting or calling my cell. I'd never had grandiose desires, never had huge dreams for fame and fortune or an exciting, adventure-filled life. All I wanted was a good job—a job that mattered, that helped people and made a difference somehow in the world—a nice home and someone I loved and who truly loved me to share my life with. Unlike most, I actually have everything I set out to find. And now something is conspiring to take it all away, and I'm not about to stand by and let that happen.

Next door, I see the light in Bruce Deacon's living room, and the faint flicker of a television. I picture him sitting there all alone, probably already drunk like he is every night, staring mindlessly at his TV but seeing only the life he'd once had and the woman he'd once shared it with. Bruce had what I have, but now it's gone. I'm sure he never saw it coming, never once suspected this would be his life—retired and alone, his wife dead and gone, his lonely days and nights one endless drunken dream—yet there it is.

"I could die tonight," he'd once told me in one of his drunken stupors. "And the world wouldn't miss a beat. It'd be like I was never even here."

With his words still rattling in my head, I leave the car and slip inside.

Remy greets me almost immediately, smiling broadly but with the subtle hint of concern I have come to recognize and love. She's already changed from her work clothes into a pair of sweatpants and a T-shirt, her hair pulled back and up into a ponytail that bounces and sways with each step.

"Hey, sweetie," she says, closing on me and wrapping me up in a big hug. "Was just about to call you and see—" Holding my shoulders, she leans back so she can look up at me in the eye. "Are you all right? You're burning up."

"Think I have a fever," I tell her as she places a palm flat against my moist forehead. "Not feeling too well."

"Yeah, you definitely do. Hang your coat up," she says, padding in her bare feet toward the downstairs bathroom. "I'll get you a couple aspirin. Going to make soup for dinner, sound good? Little chicken noodle, maybe?"

"Yeah, great," I say, though my stomach is still upset from my earlier gorging.

Once I've made my way to the couch and sat down, Remy reappears with two aspirin and a bottle of water. "Down the hatch," she says, waiting until I've swallowed both and had a long drink of water to follow it with: "Where were you?"

Much as I don't want to get into it, I also don't want to lie to her if I don't have to. "Shelly called."

Remy makes a face like she smells something bad. "Yikes."

"Yeah," I say quietly.

"Is she okay?"

"Shelly's never okay," I remind her. "She was stuck in this dump in Everett."

"For God's sake, the woman needs to get some help, Cam."

"She's been to rehab twice, didn't take."

"So what happened?"

"Went and picked her up, brought her home, told her to get some help and stop calling me whenever she's in trouble. You know, typical Shelly outing."

Remy leans in and kisses my forehead. "You're a good man."

"No, you're a good woman."

"Well, I'm patient and miraculously understanding," she says, laughing lightly. "Let's go with that."

I take her waist in my hands and gaze up at her lovingly. "I'm sorry, Rem. I know it upsets you and you have every right to feel that way. I'm just going to ignore her calls from now on, all right? Maybe just block her number or something. This has to stop and—I should've put a stop to it a long time ago. I can't keep rescuing her whenever she gets herself into these jams. She's not my responsibility anymore."

"Sit and rest," she tells me with a loving gaze of her own. "I'll go put the soup on and we'll have a nice quiet evening, okay?"

"Sure."

Once I'm alone in the great room, I see visions of the man's face I battered in the bar, and wonder what Remy would think of me if she knew what I'd done. She'd be appalled, as I am—even more so—and wouldn't understand why I'd needed to resort to violence. Truth is I didn't have to. I wanted to. And that's worse, because it's even less like me. Or is it? I'm beginning to wonder if I even know myself as well as I think I do.

Tired but restless, I force myself from the couch and walk to the small bar on the far wall alongside the window. I pour myself a scotch and carefully bring it to my parched lips as I study the framed photographs arranged in neat rows on the wall above the bar. Our wedding picture catches my eye first, a great shot of us standing on the beach where we were married, beaming on the happiest day of our lives. Then I lock on the picture of my parents, both gone now but so alive in that photograph, sitting posed and holding hands, smiling for the camera. I reach out and lightly touch the smallest of the set, a black-and-white photo of myself as a little boy playing outside the apartment where I'd been raised. So many memories, so many—

Lies.

I spin around, searching the room behind me and trying to see beyond into the kitchen. No one's there, only Remy moving about in the kitchen, preparing dinner and humming along with the radio, oblivious to the voices in my head and the horrors stalking me.

I throw back my drink in a single gulp and set the glass down on the bar.

As the liquor burns through me, calming me, I scrutinize the room, my eyes moving slowly from one corner to the next, sliding up one wall and down another. "Why are you doing this to me?" I whisper to nothing.

Silence answers.

Again, I look to the photo of me as a young boy. It seems so very long ago, my childhood.

That's because it's a lie.

"No," I whisper to thin air, chest heaving with each breath, "you're the lie."

On shaky legs, I return to the couch and sink down onto it, afraid to close my eyes because I know all I'll see are other faces staring back at me, an endless parade of bloody grimacing faces, growling and wailing in agony, their slimy jaws snapping like rabid dogs and set to a chorus of hideously diseased laughter. And fire. All around them, the most striking and depraved fire I have ever seen. And then it's gone, slinking away in a wisp like a slow spiral of smoke coiling and snaking its way toward a ceiling.

As Remy calls to me from the kitchen, asking what I'd like to drink with my soup, I realize I've just seen these horrible things anyway.

And this time with my eyes wide open.

CHAPTER FIVE

While Remy does the dishes, I stand at the sliders and watch the night consume our backyard. As darkness falls over the fire pit and the empty chairs surrounding it, I wonder if the young man only comes to me in the morning. I have never seen him at any other time, but can't be sure if that's because he isn't there or I haven't been looking.

"By the way," Remy says from the kitchen, "forgot to tell you, Cliff called again."

The sound of her voice snaps me back. I join her, grab a dish towel and begin drying and putting the dishes away. "Did he leave a message?"

"No, I spoke with him. You really need to call him back. He asked if you were mad about something, said he's been trying to reach you for more than a week and that the guys have been asking for you since you haven't made it to poker night in a while."

My friends and I all get together once a week for poker night, and have for years, but I've missed the last few outings. "Just haven't been into it lately," I confess.

"I know, but that's no reason not to return his calls or to duck him, sweetie. Cliff's your best friend. He's worried about you."

"Just been busy with work, distracted, I guess."

"Why don't you give him a call now?" Remy suggests.

"Maybe once we finish the dishes."

"Go ahead, sweetie, I can finish these up."

"You sure?"

"Absolutely, go."

"Okay, thanks." I toss the dishrag on the counter and grab the cordless phone from the wall. With the warnings of being watched through it whispering in my head, I drift back into the great room. Cliff answers on the second ring. "Hey, man."

"Hey," Cliff says tentatively. "Jesus, been calling you for days, left you a butt load of messages, thanks for calling me back, dick-weed."

"Sorry, I've just had a lot of crazy shit going on at work."

"Everything all right?"

"I'm on paid leave, actually."

"Something happen?"

I figure this is my chance to talk with him, to confide in someone about what's going on. If I don't do it now, I may not get another chance before...before what? But I can't do it here, not with Remy home. "What are you doing right now?" I ask.

"Sitting on the couch watching *Wheel of Fortune*, bored out of my tits."

"Up for a quick drink?"

"Where and when?"

Once we've made plans I disconnect, then inspect the phone, staring into it as if expecting to see some tiny creature watching me from inside the receiver. But nothing appears out of the ordinary, so I return it to its perch on the kitchen wall.

"Honey, I'm going to run out and have a drink with Cliff, okay?"

Remy puts the last glass from the sink in the drainer and wipes her soapy hands on the towel I left on the counter. "Are you sure that's a good idea tonight?"

"We need to talk. It'll just be a quick one."

She comes closer, places her hand on my forehead. "You're still a little warm."

"I'll be okay."

"You should probably go to bed early and get some sleep, Cam."

"I know." I lean down and give her a quick kiss on the lips. "But you were right, Cliff's worried about me, and talking on the phone isn't going to cut it. Figured we'd go someplace quiet, have a quick drink and chat awhile, that's all."

"Okay, but please don't be late. I have to work tomorrow."

"Just go to bed if you need to. Don't wait up, I'll be fine."

She smiles as if I should know better. "I can never sleep when you're out of the house."

"I won't be late. I promise."

Remy hops up on her tiptoes and kisses me back. "Go, have fun then—but not too much fun—and tell Cliff I said hey."

* * *

Night is in full swing as I venture toward Cliff's home base of Braintree, a suburb located just south of Boston. Situated between I-93, which leads toward the greater Boston area, and Route 3, which follows the south shore and leads to Cape Cod, it's not a long drive for me, but enough to clear my head.

Only a minute or so off the exit, O'Callahan's Bar & Grill is a sports bar and restaurant we've frequented for years. I remember in our thirties, when Cliff and I played on the same team in a local softball league, we often went to O'Callahan's after the games for beer and pizza, or their delicious assortment of appetizers. Those memories, pleasant and initially so vivid, fade then swirl away, swallowed by night, and though I desperately want to hold on to them a while longer, they're gone before I can stop them.

I pull into the lot, park, then go in through the bar entrance.

GREG F. GIFUNE

The restaurant section is busy but the bar area (all garish TVs, pendants, signed memorabilia and framed photos of sports stars) is relatively empty. Cliff is already there and sitting in a booth along the wall. Dressed in jeans, sneakers and a Boston Bruins sweatshirt, he sees me, smiles and waves me over.

"Thanks for coming out," I say, fist-bumping with him as I slide into the bench across from him.

"No problem. You okay?"

I have no idea how to answer that, but thankfully, a cheery waitress appears as if from nowhere. I order a beer and she scurries away. "I don't know, I—I need to talk."

He tries to play it cool, as Cliff always does, but his face registers concern. Running a hand up over his bald head and down across the side of his face, his fingers come to rest on his goatee. "Is everything all right with you and Remy?"

"Yeah, that's—no—everything's fine with us." I lean forward, place my elbows on the table and rub my tired eyes. "It's not that."

"Okay," he says with uncertainty. "What's up then?"

"Lately things have been...*crazy*..."

"Been worried about you, man," Cliff tells me, the irony of my statement lost on him, and why wouldn't it be? "The guys too, you haven't made a poker night in I can't remember when, and no one's heard from you."

"Apologize to everybody for me, would you? I've been busy with work and—"

"Yeah, you said you were on paid leave? What the hell's that all about?"

I give him the condensed version of Copeland's complaint and the subsequent action taken by Roz. "So now they want me to have a psych evaluation and a general physical before they can clear me to go back to work."

Cliff shakes his head and sits back. "Got to love our system, don't you? A guy that fucks little kids files a complaint and you have to have a psych evaluation. Classic."

"It's procedure."

"Bullshit is what it is. What's beyond me is why these pieces

75

of garbage are even out on the streets in the first place. Call me nuts, but you fuck with—oh, I don't know—how about *one* child, and you go bye-bye forever. Problem solved."

I don't necessarily disagree, but this is not what I've come to discuss with him, so I let it go. Bar and restaurant sounds fill the void for a moment or two.

"Besides," he says, "you're a goddamn hero. That's no way to treat you."

A few years back, I had a registrant that was acting peculiarly, and I had a gut feeling that he was about to reoffend. I staked out his house, logged his behavior and discovered he'd begun following an eleven-year-old boy home from school with his friends. It was reported to the police, and they began surveillance. Two days later they were able to stop him as he attempted to abduct the little boy from his front yard.

"Just my job," I tell him. "You do a lot of good yourself."

As a social worker, Cliff impacts the lives of many people on a regular and positive basis. Married for nineteen years, he and his wife Gloria, an RN, have an eighteen-year-old son and a thirteen-year-old daughter. Although he often bitches and complains about his family, Cliff would be lost without them. "Yeah, but if it weren't for you, that kid probably wouldn't even be alive today," he reminds me.

Thankfully, the waitress arrives with my beer, another for Cliff and a plate of hot wings. After placing them all on the table, she bops away.

"I figured you might want to split some wings," Cliff says.

"I'm all set, thanks, had dinner with Rem." I take a long sip of beer.

He pulls a few napkins from a holder on the table. "Okay, more for me."

"To be honest," I tell him, "the way things are going lately, I think the psych evaluation might be a good idea."

He looks at me as if I've spoken a language he doesn't quite grasp. "Seriously?"

I nod. "There are a lot of things going on that...things that just don't...they don't make sense, Cliff."

"Like what?"

Hesitant and still not certain how much I want to reveal to him, I ask, "Do you ever feel like…like maybe you're not yourself?"

"Sure, everybody does from time to time."

"That's not what I mean." I take another swig of beer. "Lately I…sometimes I feel like I'm not completely in…*control*."

"Of yourself or…?"

"It's as if someone else is there," I say, already aware of how ridiculous I sound. "I know it's me but…but it's like someone else takes over."

Cliff furrows his brow. "Someone else."

"Yeah."

"Takes over."

"Yes."

He grabs a wing, but says nothing.

"Things have been happening that I can't explain," I say.

The chicken poised in front of his mouth, with a sigh he lowers it and says, "Dude, I'm doing my best here, but you're going to have to be a little more specific."

"Do you believe in God?"

He shrugs. "I guess."

"No. Do you believe in God?"

He takes a bite of chicken. "I don't believe in the old guy with the long white beard sitting in a giant chair up in the clouds, if that's what you mean. But I believe in a higher power. I think there's a design to the universe, a purpose, and a consciousness behind it, if you want to call it that. But who knows?"

"What about the Devil?"

A smile slowly breaks out across Cliff's face, and then quickly fades as he realizes my question is a serious one. "No, man, I don't believe in the Devil. Or the Easter Bunny or—"

"But if there's a God, then doesn't there have to be a Devil too?"

"No. Why do people always say that? Why can't there just be a God?"

"Because everything has an opposite and—"

"Says who? Maybe God doesn't have one. Maybe there's just God, and the bad in the world is in us."

"Not bad, *evil*."

"Okay then, evil. So?"

"So you do believe in it then, regardless of source?"

"I suppose so. But what's your point? I didn't think you even believed in God."

"I don't," I say quietly. "Or at least I never did. Not really."

He drops his wing, wipes his mouth and sits back. "Then what the hell are we talking about?"

I sit back too. "I don't know," I sigh. "I'm not sure."

"Look," he says evenly, "just like you, I talk to and evaluate people and their situations for a living, all right? Just tell me what this is all about."

I draw a deep breath, and speak as I exhale. "Either something is happening to me, something very real and very...*evil*... or I...I'm losing my mind, losing my grip on reality." Even as the words fall from my mouth, the emotion begins to throttle me and I feel my eyes growing moist. I look away and quickly wipe them with the heel of my palm. "Sorry, been under a lot of stress lately."

"Hey, you don't apologize to me, man. I'm your best friend." He reaches across the table, awkwardly pats my hand, then slides the plate of chicken aside. "Just tell me what's happening, Cam, straight up."

I grab a napkin and angrily finish wiping my eyes. Why am I so emotional? "There's something wrong with me...something wrong in me...something evil."

Cliff stares at me as if he's just then seeing me for the first time. His expression and demeanor indicate gravity. "Like *The Exorcist* type shit, is that where you're going with this?"

I shrug. "I don't know."

"If you tell me my mother sucks cock in Hell and your head starts spinning around, I'm leaving, just so you know," he says with a forced chuckle. "And don't go vomiting pea soup all over the place, all right? I hate pea soup. At least make it minestrone or something good."

I glare at him.

"You're fucking serious?"

"You know I am."

He sits forward, looks around conspiratorially, then lowers his voice and says, "You're talking about *demonic possession*?"

"I'm seeing things, Cliff. Hearing things…voices…I'm doing things I wouldn't normally do, I…" My voice trails off to nothing, leaving me feeling empty and insane.

"That shit's not real."

"Are you sure?"

"Aren't you?"

"I was a couple weeks ago. Now, I don't know."

"You're an educated man." He nervously rubs his goatee, combing the hair with his fingers. "You're one of the brightest people I know. You can't believe that. You have to know that sort of thing isn't real."

"I'm not sure what's real and what isn't anymore," I admit softly.

Cliff cranes his neck, looking for our waitress. Once he locates her, he signals for another round of beers, then returns his attention to me. "Okay, all right, we—I've got this, we—we're going to discuss this rationally and intelligently like two grown men, and we're going to figure this out. We're going to line this all up and knock them down one at a time, okay?"

I nod but am hardly convinced.

"Tell me everything."

After the waitress delivers two fresh beers, calmly as I can, I explain about the young man in the yard, the homeless man and what I saw expelled from his eye, about how I saw the same type of creature moving under the sheet at Shelly's apartment, about the writing on the bathroom mirror, the visions of bloodied knuckles that came true, the horrific visions and agonizing cries of Hell, and the voices laughing and whispering in growls and tortured howls to me that my life is a lie. Then I tell him about the strange temperature drop in the house, the strange experience and lack of memory regarding what happened at Copeland's apartment, the beating I gave the man at the bar and how the young man had apparently warned me about it well before it happened, and finally, the ravenous eating spell. Hearing it all myself, I know that if it were Cliff telling me these things, I'd assume he was either crazy or outright lying, but he sits there patiently, listening and occasionally sipping his beer, offering no reaction and refraining from comment until I've finished.

"Let's start with what you've seen," he finally responds. "This guy in your yard isn't a hallucination because hallucinations don't leave physical evidence behind, which he did with the cigarettes. So this is a real person who obviously knows you or knows of you through someone else. I'd say he's potential-ly dangerous because he could be connected through one of your registrants, and with the whole watching you through the phone thing he clearly sounds like a loon, so if he appears on your property again, or if you see him anywhere near you, I say you call the police immediately and let them handle it. Bottom line, if he's on your property uninvited, then he's trespassing."

"But how did he know what was going to happen at the bar?" I ask.

"He didn't, Cam. He guessed, or he meant something else, or it's a coincidence."

"But—"

"Now the homeless guy, I think odds are there's a perfectly reasonable explanation for that, too. He's homeless, God only knows what kind of filth and disease the guy's dealing with. Maybe he really did have a maggot on his face, is that really so farfetched?"

"It came out of his eye," I remind him. "It was bigger than any maggot I've—"

"Okay, it was in his eye. Again, is that such a stretch? And maybe because you were upset and already paranoid and stressed out of your mind, you saw something bigger or worse than it actually was. Happens all the time, dude."

"But I saw the same thing at Shelly's."

"No, you saw something moving under the sheet, something

that startled and frightened you and that just as easily could've been the cat, or her adjusting her position and shifting the sheet in a way that made it look like—"

"It came out from under the sheet," I insist. "I saw it."

"Did you really, though? Or maybe did you see something you couldn't explain or weren't sure of, and fear and confusion set in and filled in the blanks, as the human mind does all the time, and due to exhaustion and stress and fear—not to mention the experience you had with the homeless guy—you saw what your mind put there to fill the space. Again, happens all the time, man. It's how our minds work, especially under high levels of stress or fear. The human mind fills spaces, choosing from a file of images and explanations it already possesses, in order to make sense of things."

I shake my head, unconvinced.

"Think about it a minute," Cliff says. "Don't those explanations seem far more reasonable and likely than what you're suggesting? And maybe when you were at this Copeland guy's place, you really did have some sort of breakdown or something. Look at what you deal with all day. I see some sad stories and people with issues all day long too, but you're dealing with some pretty horrific stuff day in and day out. Just the case files you have to read alone are enough to do psychological damage to anyone over time. Maybe it just all caught up to you, man, and you needed a break and didn't take one and something had to give."

He has a point there. "What about the rest?" I ask.

"The writing on the mirror, the sounds and visions and the whole bloody knuckles thing, in my mind, can be chalked up to the condition you're in. You're exhausted and stressed. Maybe you're depressed and don't even realize it. I'm not saying there may not be chemical issues here—who knows—I'm not a doctor, I'm just saying I think there are clearly issues you're dealing with right now, and they're emotional and psychological ones, Cam, not real experiences, though they obviously seem real to you in the moment. It could also explain the violence you took out on the asshole at the bar and the whole gorging on food thing. When people are under tremendous amounts of stress and also dealing with exhaustion, they do and see and hear strange things. It's really not that unusual. Now obviously this sounds excessive, but that's why they have shrinks, my friend. You're right, the psych evaluation is a good idea, and not because you're insane or losing your mind. It doesn't have to be that extreme, okay? It just doesn't. People suffer from emotional and minor psychological issues all the time, there's no shame in it and it doesn't mean they're crazy. Sometimes chemicals in our brains can just be a little off, and maybe with some meds or whatever, a qualified psychiatrist can get things leveled off again where they need to be. I'm telling you, man, that's all this is. Once you go talk to someone, get some serious rest and let them help you get this back under control, you'll be fine. The last thing you want to do is freak out or buy into the fear, okay? All that's going to do is continue to confuse you and make you feel like you can't distinguish between reality and bullshit. Level heads prevail, right? So that's what you need to focus on, staying as level as you can."

Everything he's said makes sense to me, and he's right, it certainly sounds more reasonable and likely than the other possibilities coursing through my brain. But even as I sit there and process that, I know he's wrong. This is something else. Something worse, because whatever it is or isn't, it's happening in reality. It's alive and moving inside me. I can feel it.

"Besides," he says, "reality's overrated. It's all perception."

I look out across the bar. Nothing seems out of place or unusual. "Not all of it."

"Let me tell you a story. When Jenny was little, I don't know, like nine or ten, she went to Gloria and told her she'd heard at school that Santa Claus wasn't real and wanted to know if that was true. So Gloria dodges the question and tells her to ask me. She does. *Is Santa real?* she asks. *Do you think he's real?* I ask her back. *Yes*, she says. *Because there's evidence of him everywhere, she says, he's on TV and in movies and in books. He's at the mall. Every*

Christmas morning there's proof he was here. I believe in him and I know he's real, she says. *You believe in him,* I say, *so you think he's real. But how do you know? How do you know he's real?* I ask. The kid looks me dead in the eye. *Because you told me he is,* she says. Bottom line, dude, reality is what we think it is, what we believe it to be, what we're told it is." Cliff kills his beer. "And when that falls apart or no longer makes sense, then we have to pick up the pieces and figure out what it all means again."

"Only problem with that story is that Santa Claus was never real."

"Wasn't he? To her he was. Think back to when you were a kid. Wasn't he as real to you as anything else?" He sighs. "You had a misstep with Shelly, but since then you've had a great life, Cam. Good job, beautiful and awesome wife, nice home—Christ, you were even smart enough not to have kids—you're living the dream. But sometimes those dreams get sidetracked, knocked offline, you know? And just like when you reboot your computer, we have to reset, get our shit straight again and figure out what's what. No shame in it. That's life. If there's a devil living inside you, it's no different from the one living inside the rest of us, and it sure as hell isn't something out of a horror movie or anything literal. We all have our demons, Cam. Usually we can outrun them, but now and then the motherfuckers catch us. It's not the end of the world, you just have to shake them off and start again. Not saying it's easy, but it's not impossible either. You ought to call Roz and ask her to get you those appointments ASAP," Cliff says. "Get it done, get your head straight, and you'll be okay. You'll see."

Cliff is doing his best, and I expect nothing less. He's always been good at calmly making sound judgments, and is extremely skilled at organizing things into neat little categories so they seem to make sense even when they may not. And as that's exactly what he's doing, I let it go and nod, doing my best to convince him that his efforts have not been in vain. He's listened and he's helped. "You're right," I concede, though I feel more alone than ever, like I'm sinking even deeper into a dark and deadly hole from which there will never be any escape. No one understands because no one's capable of it. It's beyond understanding and comprehension because it's beyond belief. But things beyond belief happen all the time, and most of us conveniently dismiss that. More handy little boxes and explanations that sound good, make sense, and should provide the answers we need. But they don't. Not always. What then? For now, I gaze up helplessly at the edge of that hole, watch sand trickle down from all sides, the dirt walls threatening to implode, collapse in and bury me at any moment. "Of course you're right. I let this get away from me and I need to rein it back in, not buy into the uncertainty and the fear."

"And another thing," he adds. "Stay away from Shelly. She's trouble, never been anything but, and she'll drag you down sure as I'm sitting here. It's what she does. It's what she's always done to you. With these other issues going on right now, she's the last thing you need in your life right now. Besides, you don't owe her shit. She's not your problem anymore. Not to mention you've got the perfect wife at home, so worry about her. Let her help you through this. She'll be there for you, Remy always is."

"I know I should, but I haven't really talked to her about it," I explain, "because I didn't want to worry or upset her."

Cliff gives me a stern look. "She can't be there for you unless you let her."

I look around, waiting for something to happen, some hideous vision or odd behavior from the patrons. But everything is as it should be. "You're right." I offer a smile I hope appears genuine. "About everything. Happy now, you smug bastard?"

"Been telling you for years I'm not just eye candy," he chuckles, signals the waitress and mouths to her that we need the bill. "But one thing I was wrong about is those appointments with the doctors. Make them soon as you can. The mind's very powerful, and it's easy to let our thoughts run wild. I'm sure you'll find none of this is as bad as it seems at the moment, but it's also nothing to take lightly, ignore or play around with. And don't play games with that kid. He comes around again, call the fuzz."

The waitress returns with our bill and Cliff asks her to wrap the wings up to go.

"Thanks for coming out," I tell him, "and putting up with me and this nonsense."

"It's not nonsense. You need to take care of yourself, that's all. I'm always here if you need me, you know that. Day or night, I got your back."

"Right back at you," I say, throwing a couple bucks down toward the bill. "And for real, thanks. But I promised Remy I wouldn't be late, so I better get back."

"Me too," he says. "If the couch doesn't fart soon, Gloria's gonna know I'm gone."

As we laugh and shake hands, I catch a glimpse of the cocky young college kid Cliff was when we met, a mischievous wiseass everyone loved. That all seems so impossibly long ago now, maybe because that's exactly what it is.

"And remember what I told you," he says, unusual intensity in his eyes. "Reality is what we think it is, what we believe it to be, what we're told it is."

Yeah, I think. *Until it isn't.*

CHAPTER SIX

I should go home. But I don't. I drive into Boston and head
for the Back Bay. The lights from the cityscape are magical, the
energy coming from them palpable even from a distance. I park
a few blocks from my office, lock the car and begin to walk
with no idea why or where I'm going. I only know I want to
walk. After a moment I realize I'm moving at such an acceler-
ated pace I'm almost running. Making a conscious effort, I slow
down as I move by South Station. It's chilly out, the air sharp
and sobering, and though it's later now, it's also a weeknight,
so this part of town is mostly quiet and deserted, the streets
empty but for the occasional walker like myself or the sporadic
appearance of a car or truck. I know this area well, yet it feels as
if I'm only vaguely familiar with it. Everything seems slightly
off, like the world itself is askew. Maybe it's gone crazy and I'm
fine. Either way, the night is liquid and alive, moving all around
me and luring me toward something else, some *other* I cannot

yet discern. It's as if every possible reality is present and occurring on this night, unfolding in unison, as one, each separated by and hidden behind the sheerest curtains of darkness.

At the corner, the bright lights of a convenience store draw my attention.

I stand outside a moment, staring at the signage in the windows and trying to remember if I've ever been inside. Probably, but doesn't matter, so I yank open the door, slip inside and head directly for the counter.

A skinny college-aged kid with unruly locks and scruffy facial hair sits behind the counter slumped on a stool and reading a dog-eared copy of Jean-Paul Sartre's *No Exit*. He glances up, and realizing I won't be grabbing anything else before approaching the counter, puts the book down with a questioning look.

"*L'enfer, c'est les autres*," I say.

"Huh?"

"*Hell is other people*," I say, motioning to his book.

"The famous Sartre quote."

"Oh." The kid nods vacantly, staring at me with empty, glassy eyes. "Yeah, I don't really speak French, homey."

I feel myself grin, but I find nothing humorous about his response. In fact, he's making me angry, far more than seems warranted. I can feel the rage rising, bubbling up toward the surface, boiling in my veins. I want to hurt him. "Let me get a pack of Marlboro box," I tell him, quickly searching the counter area until I find a display of disposable lighters. I grab one and place it on the counter between us. "And this."

He reaches up to a large case suspended above him and pulls a pack of cigarettes free. After scooping up the lighter, he scans them both, then returns them to the counter and mumbles what I owe him.

I pay while trying desperately to ignore the sudden desire to grab him by his pencil-neck and slam his stupid fucking apathetic face into the counter. I can almost hear the sound of his teeth breaking off at the root, can almost see the blood flowing.

And it's wonderful.

What the hell is the matter with me?

Before it gets any worse, I snatch up my items and hurry out the door.

Once outside it occurs to me that I haven't smoked a cigarette in ages. I smoked when I was married to Shelly, but quit a long time ago. Quitting was so awful, and I felt so much better once I got through it, I've never had a desire to smoke again. Until tonight, when it feels as if I've never stopped.

Rather than paying attention to where I'm going, my focus is on unwrapping the pack, tearing it open and lighting up a cigarette as quickly as possible. Suddenly it feels as if I'm in the throes of the worst nicotine fit I've ever experienced.

I hesitate. I can't. I don't want to start smoking again.

Just smoke one, you fucking pussy. Do it. Do it now.

At the corner I fumble a cigarette free and fire it up. Inhaling greedily, I take a long and violent pull. The smoke burns the back of my throat and sets my lungs on fire as I hack out the first drag. Undeterred, I take hit after hit until I can inhale deeply without coughing. My head spins and my chest wheezes like a chew toy just like it did when I had a two-pack-a-day habit, yet it feels good to me. It feels *right*.

Disgusted with myself, I flick the cigarette away, stuff the pack and lighter into my pocket and keep moving. *Wait. Where the hell am I?* Apparently at some point I took a side street or alley, because I find myself in a neighborhood I'm unfamiliar with and to my knowledge have never been to. Consisting of abandoned warehouses and largely unused commercial space, it is deathly quiet, and most of the buildings on either side of the street sit dark and vacated. There aren't even streetlights here, but as I walk on, at the next block I see a faint red glow seeping through the darkness from a set of stairs that lead below street level. Once closer, I see that the light comes from a modest sign above a door at the base of the steps that reads: AMORPHOUS LOUNGE.

Before I realize it, I'm down the steps and pushing through the door.

The place is small and intimate with lighting so limited it takes my eyes several seconds to adjust. Once they do, I realize no one is here. All the tables are empty, and the stage at the rear of the club is dark and quiet. The bar on the far wall is stocked with an array of the finest liquors and nicely backlit, but there are no patrons, only a male bartender in a black tuxedo manically wiping down the already pristine counter. Just inside the door stands a host's podium. As if on cue, a maître d' type appears from the darkness behind it. Also dressed in a black tuxedo, his dark hair is slicked back and held in place with a generous amount of hair gel, his moonlike face gaunt and badly pockmarked, eyes beady, black and small, like a rat's. He bows formally, just coming up short of clicking his heels together.

"Good evening, sir," he says, voice smooth and laced with a slight European accent, "how very nice to see you."

"Are you open?" I ask.

He presents a smile that is either accommodating or condescending, I can't be sure which. "We're always open, Mr. Horne."

My blood runs cold. "How do you know my name?"

"You're such the jokester, sir." The man laughs politely. "I know your name because you're a regular, of course."

I have never set foot in this place before, and have never laid eyes on this man.

"Would you like your regular table, Mr. Horne?"

Mystified, I stand there nodding idiotically, my mouth dry as sand.

The maître d' leads me through the numerous empty tables, each outfitted with expensive white linen and a single candle in the center encased in intricate red glass globes, some burning but most extinguished. As we arrive at a table directly in front of the stage, he bows and sweeps his hand at my chair with a grand motion so over-the-top it would be comical were it not so creepy.

As I sit, the man slides the chair in gently behind me. "Will you be having a drink this evening, sir?"

"Yes," I manage. "Please."

"Right away, Mr. Horne," he says, then before I can tell him what I want, turns on his heel and glides away toward the bar.

Before me is a small, dark and empty stage. It seems out of place to me, as it is dusty and old, unlike the rest of the place which, while dated, is immaculate to the point that I wonder if any of it's ever been used before tonight.

A glass and small napkin slide onto the table before me as the maître d' delivers my drink. I take a sip and it feels good on my parched and sore throat. Vodka and cranberry juice, not my usual drink, but he seems to think it is.

"I hope it's to your liking, sir."

"Thank you, it's fine," I say quietly. "What is your name?"

He smiles again, but this time it looks almost evil, partially hidden in the shadows beyond the reach of the candlelight on my table, his black eyes piercing even in scarce light. "You know my name just as well as you know your own, Mr. Horne."

"Humor me."

"Why, it's Anthony, of course."

"Of course," I say. "Forgive me, Anthony. I'm afraid I haven't been myself lately."

"I certainly hope your time with us here will help you with that, sir. Will there be anything else for the time being?"

"No. Thank you, Anthony, that will be all for now."

With a formal nod, he retreats to his podium near the entrance.

A loud sound shatters the silence, a toggle being thrown, and suddenly a spotlight appears on the stage before me. I have another sip of my drink. It's delicious, the best cocktail I've ever had. I notice a small glass ashtray on the table, so I dig my cigarettes from my pocket and light one. Unlike earlier, the cigarette is smooth and tastes great.

A strange squeaking noise echoes through the room as vines of smoke spiral around me and snake through the spotlight. Two men dressed in white appear from the darkness at the rear of the stage. Looking like attendants from a mental hospital, they wheel out an old industrial-style bed with a rusty iron frame and position it in the center of the stage. Without a word, they fade back into the darkness from which they came.

After a moment, a man emerges from the darkness and cross-es the stage. Barefoot, he wears a long black satin robe, the hood pulled up and over his head to hide his face. Still as stone, he stands next to the bed, head bowed. From behind him, a woman, also barefoot and dressed in a satin robe—this one red—walks into the spotlight and stands on the opposite side of the bed. A hood covers her bowed head as well.

Silence returns until the steady thump of a drum and the smooth whisper of cymbals can be heard, the music evidently piped in through hidden speakers all around me. As the music begins, the man peels back his hood, then opens his robe and drops it to the floor. He is completely nude, his pale, plump and hairy body pockmarked with cellulite and patches of red and irritated skin. Bald but for sprigs of unwashed and unruly hair jutting out from either side of his head, he remains motionless and keeps his head bowed, but I know now who it is.

Alfred Copeland.

Taking a final angry drag on my cigarette, I crush it in the ashtray as the woman follows suit, peeling back her hood, then dropping the robe to the floor. Nude as well, the moment my eyes move to her, I realize I know that body well. I've touched and tasted every inch of it. Refusing to look at me, Remy climbs onto the bed and lies on her back, her movement robotic and her face void of expression.

I spring to my feet, but before I can charge the stage I feel an unusually strong hand on my shoulder, and suddenly Anthony is there, standing next to me and holding me in place. "Come now, Mr. Horne," he says evenly, gently pushing me back down into my chair. "You know how this works."

Helpless, I watch as Copeland climbs onto the bed and Remy spreads her legs to accommodate him. He glides into her, his dimpled and scarred buttocks pumping as he fucks her, his dan-gling and jiggling gut slapping her belly and breasts. Both remain expressionless—neither lustful nor disgusted—their movements mechanical and lifeless as they switch positions and he begins slamming into her from behind.

I power down the remainder of my drink, then smash the glass down on the table.

Remy's small breasts jump, bouncing in time with Copeland's increasingly violent thrusts.

"Stop this," I tell Anthony, my anger giving way to crippling sadness, a level of sorrow I have never before experienced. "Please. Stop this, I—"

"That which has been preordained cannot be *stopped*," Anthony says, powerful grip still clamped on my shoulder. "And who should know that better than you?"

Copeland grabs Remy's waist, his thick hands and sausage-like fingers sinking into her soft flesh as he pumps harder. Their bodies, slick with sweat, slap against each other even harder. The nauseating sound it produces nearly drowns out his grunts and groans, until he empties himself inside her, crying out as if mortally wounded. Sated, he collapses onto her with his full weight. Lying atop her, his ample girth rising and falling in rapid succession, he gasps for breath as drool escapes his mouth in a long string and trickles down the back of Remy's neck.

Finally, Copeland rolls off her, his flesh jiggling and pasty. He slides from the bed, regains his feet, and still without looking at me, turns back and takes hold of his wet and now flaccid member.

An arc of urine shoots through the air as Remy rolls onto her back, spattering across her belly, chest and face. She lies there without protest, staring up at the dark ceiling like a corpse.

Once finished, Copeland turns and gazes out at the empty tables and chairs, never looking at me, and bows like an actor at a curtain call.

Anthony finally releases me and begins to clap maniacally. "Bravo! Bravo!"

Copeland takes Remy's hand and helps her from the bed. She stands next to him, dipping sweat, cum and urine, then bows too, her expression still lifeless and flat.

"Brava!" Anthony shouts, clapping even harder. "Brava!"

The music stops. Remy and Copeland bow their heads and the spotlight disappears, the darkness swallowing them whole.

So cold now, as if long dead myself, I point at the stage. "I'm going to kill him. You know that, don't you?"

"You're so silly tonight, Mr. Horne," Anthony says, smiling at me with his demonic grin and soulless black eyes. "You already have."

* * *

My drink, there...there's something in my drink...

"What do you want with Remy? Why would you involve her in this? Whatever this is about, it has nothing to do with her. Let her go, leave her alone, she's never done anything to anyone. Leave her out of it. Whatever I've done, I—obviously it's me you want, not her—I, just leave her alone. I'm the luckiest man in the world, she—she's the kindest, most loving, intelligent, loyal and patient human being I have ever known. A perfect mate, a flawless wife, I could not love her more than I do and she—just leave her alone..."

"You've no need to be concerned with that right now, Mr. Horne. You have more important things to worry about."

I try to see Anthony's face but it's gone now, it's...it's become something else, his black eyes bottomless pits, pestilent caverns, passageways to another place and time, another reality...

Where is he taking me? Where are we going?

Holding me tight by the arm, he leads me deeper into darkness... lower...beneath the nightclub and into the sewers and shadows, where unclean things watch from the darkness, the filthy dripping darkness...

I have never felt so alone, so goddamn alone.

"Help me..."

I don't want to go where he's taking me...I...I'm afraid...there are things here, clinging to the curved and cavernous walls and ceilings, floating and swimming in the dirty water, waiting in the filth... horrible things...frightening things...

"None more frightening than you, sir."

"What have I done? God help me, what have I done?"

"You don't believe in God," Anthony reminds me.

"But He believes in you."

The water is deeper now, up beyond my knees and—and I can feel things moving in it—brushing up against me and—biting—they're biting they—they're biting me, tearing chunks of flesh from my legs, dropping me down as Anthony releases me and…and I'm sinking… sinking into this horrible water that smells like death and feces and blood.

"He believes in your blasphemy…He believes in your betrayal…"

I cannot stop it, I—please—I'm sinking lower, the water splashing up over my face, my mouth and nostrils, the sewers so dark I can't see anything.

"So do we…and it's beautiful…"

Down. Down. I cannot see, but I can feel. Down beneath the filthy water I fall.

Broken…by my master.

* * *

The sun slowly rises, breaking over the trees as night burns away, taking my nightmares along with it. At least for now.

I have no memory of driving home. All I know is once I got here, I ran into the house like a madman, bounded up the stairs to our bedroom and checked on Remy to make sure she was all right. She was still awake, but barely, under the covers and dozing with the television on. When she saw me, she smiled, so beautiful and free of all the darkness and horror I'd been lost in. Still fully dressed, I crawled into bed with her, kissed her, held her in my arms and whispered how much I loved and needed her.

"Have you been smoking?" she asked blearily. "Your breath smells like cigarettes."

"It's all right. Go back to sleep, my love."

Later, once she had, I left her there, went downstairs, made myself a drink, then went out to the backyard. Sitting in one of the Adirondack chairs, I waited, watching for the sun and the return of the young man.

And return he does.

My eyes close. Perhaps I nap for a moment or two, I can't be sure, but when I open my eyes, there he is, sitting in the other chair just feet from me with the same sad face and disheveled look he always has. And in the distance, through the trees, the phantom car alarm begins to wail.

"No more games," I say. "What's happening to me?"

He stares at the ground, and in his whispery voice says, "They gather when something bad is about to happen. They wait and watch, like they're doing now. Slowly, they get stronger. Eventually, they usher it in. They don't make it happen. They're just there to help it along. Same way sharks swim to blood."

"Sharks are more than ushers. They're predators."

"So are they."

"Who are they?"

"Not who," he says, "*what*."

"What then. What are they?"

He glances at me with his sad, teary eyes. "Exactly what you think they are, what you're afraid they are, what your mind tells you they can't be."

"I'm changing."

"I know."

"Can I stop this? Can I stop them?"

He looks away.

"What's your name?" I ask him.

He seems baffled by the question. "Call me Mac."

"How do you fit into all this? Are you ever going to answer that? Who are you?"

Standing, he lights a cigarette, leaves it dangling between his lips, then gazes out at the forest behind us. "You'll see."

I watch as he wanders out of the yard and into the trees. And then he's gone.

Head in my hands, I rub my temples as the cries of the distant car alarm drone on, splintering the slowly breaking dawn of a new day.

CHAPTER SEVEN

The rain brings me back. Running, spraying, spattering, dripping from the eaves of the house and gushing through the gutters, it is alive and vibrant and speaks to me like the ghosts in my head, whispering in ancient and long-dead languages I will never decipher. Yet I understand. On a level primal in its simplicity and pure in its raw fear, I understand. There is no escape from what's happening. Running away from it will only destroy me faster. I must run *toward* it, straight into its teeth, and confront it with every fiber of my being if I'm to have even the slightest chance of survival.

Although it is morning, the rain and storm clouds leave the house unusually dark. Without bothering to turn on a light, I sit on the edge of the couch in the great room, lowering myself onto it gradually like a slowly deflating balloon. Having been born and raised in the city, this quiet and modest house in a cozy small town has always represented my dream. Until recently, this house and this life has been a dream, a dream come true. But I'm coming to despise that word. Dream. So innocuous yet so devastating, as this place now feels more like a prison, a place I want to flee from whenever possible, because maybe if I'm not here, then none of the darkness stalking me will be either, and Remy and everything else I care about will be safe again.

I can hear Remy moving around upstairs, preparing for work, and I feel safer somehow, connected to her in ways I cannot even begin to comprehend, much less explain. I only know I love her so much it hurts, and that this is where I belong.

You belong with us…

"No," I say aloud, my voice foreign and odd in the otherwise silent room.

The rain saves me a second time, once more bringing me back and away from the fires burning in my mind. Back. Maybe that's the key. I have to go back. Back to before this all began, back to the beginning, when things first changed, because that's where the answers to this mystery lie. They must.

Alfred Copeland, I think. *Everything changed after I went to that bastard's apartment.*

Remy comes down the stairs like a vision, showered and rested and ready for work, bouncing with each step and happy as can be.

It rained that day at Copeland's apartment too.

"So glad you got together with Cliff and worked things out," she says, giving me a quick peck on the cheek before hurrying into the kitchen. "He was worried about you."

"Yeah, everything's fine."

Liar…

"Oh, and don't forget, that thing at Sue and Dario's is tonight," she calls from the other room.

"What thing?"

Remy pokes her head around the door frame. "They're having a get-together, just a small cocktail party at their place. We talked about it last week, remember?"

"No, I—sorry—no, I forgot."

"We're still going, right?" she asks hopefully.

"I don't know, Rem. Not sure I'm up for it, to be honest."

She frowns playfully. "I kinda sorta already told them we were coming."

"I haven't been feeling well lately, and with being off work and all, I…"

Remy crosses the room, squats before me and takes my hands in hers. "Sitting in this house all day and night is the last thing you need to do, sweetie. Maybe getting out and mixing with other people and having some fun would do you a world of good. Might be just what you need. It's just a harmless little cocktail party."

I smile for her like a puppet, force away visions of her on that stage, her legs spread in the spotlight. Bile gurgles at the back of my throat. "Maybe," I tell her. "We'll see how I feel when you get home from work, okay?"

"Okay." She kisses my hands, then brushes them tenderly against her cheek, holding them there a moment.

Behind her, through the rain-blurred windows, I see something large, dark and similar to a human being watching us. It shifts, moves and begins to quake, trembling at impossible speeds. Then it's gone, absorbed by the storm.

Or maybe it was never there at all.

As a chill prances across the back of my neck, I tell Remy I love her, but find myself wondering if I really know her as well as I think I do. And does she know me?

I know you, Horne. I know you.

Remy's eyes sparkle. "I love you too," she says.

I can only hope that's enough.

* * *

The rain has gotten heavier by the time I arrive in Boston. Parked a few blocks from the office, I sit in the car watching the rain sluice along the windshield and windows. The steady drum of raindrops echoes off the roof and hood, making me feel safe and protected within my cocoon of plastic, steel and glass. I embrace it, listen to the rain and watch it wash over the car as my thoughts shift to Alfred Copeland.

In time, I dial Marianne Feeney's cell. She answers on the third ring.

"It's me," I tell her.

"Cam, hi—hey—how are you?"

"I need a favor. My work account's been frozen so I can't access our site or any registrant files." Ghostly apparitions glide beyond the rain-blurred windows, phantoms disguised as passersby and traffic. "And I need to get into one."

"Um, okay," she says, her nervousness evident. "Which file?"

"A registrant named Alfred Copeland."

Marianne breathes heavily into the phone. "Isn't he the one that made the complaint against you?"

"Yeah, that's him."

"Do you really think it's a good idea to do that with all that's—"

"I just need some information. I'll go through it real quick, in and out, okay? If I go in through your account, no one will ever know."

"What is it you're looking for?" she asks.

"I want to read his file again, what's the big deal?"

"Well, if you tell me exactly what you need, I could go in for you and—"

"Goddamn it!" Rage explodes through me with no warning, and I grip the steering wheel with such force my knuckles go white. "Enough with the interrogation, I need your fucking help!"

"Jesus," she says. "Calm down."

I struggle to maintain my composure but everything is raw and fierce, coursing through me and beyond my control. "I—look—I don't have a lot of time, understand? Either you're willing to help me or you're not. Which is it?"

"Of course I'll help you if I can. Take it easy. I know you're having some issues right now but I—I mean—why would you speak to me like that?"

Deep breaths, one after another, slowly weaken the anger. "I'm sorry. Really, I am, I'm sorry. But I need to see that file."

"Okay, but I'm not in the office," she confesses. "I'm in the field and on my way to an appointment. But when I'm done I can—"

"Got your laptop with you?"

"Of course, but listen—"

"Where are you? I'll meet you."

* * *

Once on Mass Ave., I follow it to the Harvard Bridge and cross the river into Cambridge. Sheets of rain soak the city, casting everything in a blurred murkiness.

It's becoming the norm, but nothing feels right.

After a few blocks, I find the street Marianne said she'd be waiting on. A narrow street populated by brownstones, it's a better neighborhood than I'd anticipated. Sometimes they are. Her Mazda is parked near the corner, but there are no available spaces, so I flick my lights at her, then turn and grab the first space I can find on the cross street.

Hurrying back through the rain, I slip into the passenger side of Marianne's car, drenched and out of breath. She waits for me behind the wheel in a skirt suit and an ankle-length raincoat, her red hair pulled up and back into a stylish nest on the top of her head. The car smells like cologne and baby powder.

"Excuse me, do I know you?" she says through a smirk.

I give her a look, then glare at the radio, which is playing a local sports talk show.

She takes the hint and shuts it off.

"Some rain, huh?" she says, her smirk morphing into a pleasant smile.

"Thanks for seeing me."

"Not like you left me a whole lot of choice there, bud." Marianne continues to smile but I can tell she's uncomfortable. "As if I wouldn't see you, don't be silly."

"I'm sorry I got so upset on the phone. I just—I'm stressed out of my mind."

She puts a hand to her cheek and does her best Jack Benny. "No!"

I shrug, embarrassed. "I didn't mean to take it out on you. I'm sorry."

"You're forgiven, I'm just playing." She taps the crystal on her wristwatch. "But like I tried to explain, I've got an appointment—unscheduled—and have to get in there."

"Can you leave your laptop?"

"No, Cam, I cannot leave my laptop. I need it for work." With a light laugh, she gathers a leather satchel containing her computer and slings it over her shoulder along with her purse. "Give me about twenty minutes, then I'll be back out and we can—"

"What's the job?"

"Change-of-address dodger," Marianne says through a sigh. "Real charmer, an investment broker with a foot fetish and a habit of groping women's feet in public. He's also a sexual sadist with a handful of arrests for domestics and a history of physical and sexual violence toward his special lady friends. From what I can tell, he buys his way out of most charges and troubles, but even someone with his bucks can't avoid the sex-offender rap once he's been convicted. Even follows his big-shot pompous ass, as it should. Anyway, he's quite the piece of work, but I won't be long, promise."

"Want me to come in with you?"

"Well, let's see. You don't technically work for the department at the moment, so it's not only unethical but illegal for you to be present. And if anyone found out, I could, and probably would, lose my job for allowing you to be there. Other than that it seems like a great idea, sure, let's go for it." She shakes her head. "Seriously, you really need to pull it together.

This is not the Cameron Horne I know."

You have no idea.

When I don't answer, she aims a fire-engine-red fingernail at a brownstone a few doors down and says, "I've got to get in there. Sit tight, I'll be back soon as I can."

I sit alone in her car awhile, listening to the rain and the vague traces of voices in my head. My leg bounces nervously and I can feel my body begin to perspire. I don't know if I've ever felt so alone.

Though I tell myself not to, I climb from the car, dash across the sidewalk and up the stairs to the brownstone Marianne entered just moments before. Except for rain sounds, the city is quiet. I look back at the empty street, the cars and other buildings. Something is watching me, something close. I can feel its eyes crawling across my skin, its thoughts burrowing into my head. I open the brownstone door and step into a small foyer, leaving the rain and the ghosts concealed within it behind me.

To my right is a staircase, to my left a short hallway leading to a door that stands ajar. I listen a moment, hear Marianne's voice, and follow it to the doorway, moving quietly as possible.

Through the cracked door, I see a kitchen and a living room beyond, nicely and expensively designed and decorated. Marianne stands on one side of a large island with her laptop on and open and her paperwork spread out across the counter. A well-dressed man in a suit and tie, who appears to be in his early thirties, stands on the opposite side of the island looking uncomfortable and annoyed. A few feet away, sitting in a chair at the kitchen table, a waif of a woman in her early twenties watches quietly.

"Exactly how long is this going to take?" the man asks.

Without looking up from her laptop, Marianne eventually replies, "Soon as we get the necessary paperwork completed, Mr. Westbrook, I'll be on my way."

"Well, if you could hurry it up, I'd appreciate it. I've got a great deal of work to do and several important appointments today." The man shakes his head and sighs. "I simply don't have time for this nonsense, for God's sake, I—"

"You're well aware of the rules and laws of the Commonwealth pertaining to your situation, Mr. Westbrook," Marianne says, finally making eye contact. "You're required by law to notify our department when you change addresses. You chose not to comply with that when you moved into your new home. As a result, I had to track you down and come to you unannounced to update your information. That's not my fault, it's yours. Now you can either cooperate and we can get this done quickly, or you can continue to be unnecessarily hostile and I'll be happy to turn this over to—"

"Hostile?" Westbrook says, his anger growing. "How am I being *hostile*?"

"I don't appreciate your tone," she tells him.

Westbrook leans on the counter, closer to her. "And I don't appreciate being harassed by you people for something that took place a thousand years ago I wasn't even guilty of. Can you appreciate that, Ms. Feeney?"

"No one's harassing you," Marianne says, returning to her paperwork. "I'm just doing my job."

"You believe this crap?" he says to the woman in the chair.

She says nothing, just stares straight ahead with her blank doe eyes. Petite and mousey, the woman is barefoot, dressed in yellow Capri pants and a sleeveless top, and looks tired and stressed well beyond someone of her meager years should be.

"I've got things to do," Westbrook snaps, "and have to get to work, so we need to move this along or I'm going to get my attorney on the phone and—"

I push the door the rest of the way open and step through into the kitchen.

Westbrook looks at me, incredulous. "Who the hell's this guy?"

I flash my ID and drift toward Marianne, but before I can say anything she announces, "This is my associate." And then, turning her back to them and glaring at me says, "I thought you were going to wait in the car."

"Decided to join you," I say with a smile, holding West-brook's beady-eyed stare throughout. "Good morning, Mr. Westbrook."

"Yeah, good morning, come right into my house uninvited, feel free."

"The door was open, sir," I tell him.

"The door to the street wasn't."

"You're mistaken."

"Yeah, okay, I get it." He turns to the woman again and jerks a thumb in my direction. "See what I mean now about these people? They think they can do whatever they want because they have some three-dollar ID from the state. They think they can treat me like scum because of a false charge from years ago."

"That would be a conviction, Mr. Westbrook, not a charge," I remind him. "And as Ms. Feeney said, we're just here to do our job. So I suggest you let us do that and we'll be out of your hair sooner than later, all right?"

"Sure, tough guy, do your thing." Westbrook anxiously straightens the cuff links on his shirtsleeves. "Let them feel like big bad officials," he says to his girlfriend. "Most of these clowns are two or three IQ points away from being meter maids, for Christ's sake. End of the day, I make what they make in a year every thirty minutes or so." He laughs, congratulating himself on what he apparently believes is his devastating wit, and though his girlfriend remains silent, a slight smile bends her thin lips as well.

After giving me another annoyed look, Marianne returns to her paperwork and asks Westbrook to sign some forms. Mean-while, I move deeper into the kitchen for a better look at the woman in the chair. She avoids eye contact with me, looking down at the floor before I get too close. I wonder how many times Westbrook has beaten her, humiliated her, sexually as-saulted her, hurt her. Why would she stay with someone like this? Why would she allow him to do these things to her?

I notice her feet are bruised and covered in scabs from what appear to be bite marks. I crouch down in front of her but she still refuses to look at me. "What's your name?" I ask.

"None of your goddamn business," Westbrook says. "Don't answer him, you—you have no right to interrogate her—you're not here for her and she's under no obligation to speak to you or answer your out-of-line questions, got it? I know my fucking rights, pal. She's none of your concern. Leave her alone or I'll file a complaint so fast it'll make your empty head spin."

"Calm down, Mr. Westbrook," Marianne says evenly but with enough force to gain his attention. "And don't threaten us or I promise you things are going to get a whole lot more complicated for you, understand?"

I nearly allow a proud smile. "Are you all right?" I ask the woman.

She nods but says nothing.

"It won't get any better," I tell her, "only worse. You know that, don't you?"

"Did you just—did he just—what the fuck? Did he actually just say that?" Westbrook stomps his way toward us. "Listen up, pal, I—"

I stand, turn and face him. "Back up."

He stops but holds his ground.

"I said, *back up*." I stare deep into his arrogant, beady little eyes, and he stares back. Within seconds, he sees something that makes him understand upsetting me further would not be a good idea, and he returns to his position behind the counter.

"Okay," Marianne says, barely able to contain her anger, "I think I've got this well in hand so, why don't you just wait for me outside? I'll be done here in just a moment."

I walk closer to the island, closer to her but also closer to Westbrook, who still stares at me, but with far less arrogance and aggression than before. There is something else in those eyes now. Fear...uncertainty...

How's it feel, asshole?

Westbrook grimaces, and it's obvious he wants to look away from me, but for some reason can't. He reminds me of a child that has just learned that the monster under his bed is not only real but far worse than he'd ever imagined.

You see it, don't you? You see this thing *inside me.*

Suddenly I feel Marianne's hand on my arm, gripping it tightly. "Go ahead outside and wait for me in the car, please."

"Hey, look," Westbrook says, stuttering as his entire demeanor changes, "I didn't, ah, mean any offense, okay? I'm all about cooperating here. I've just got a busy day ahead of me and I wasn't expecting all this and—you know what, though?—that's not your fault or problem, so I apologize if I've offended either of you in any way or made this more difficult than it needs to be. I'm happy to cooperate fully so we can all get on with our day. You guys are just doing your jobs. I'm sorry for being so difficult. I was out of line."

Marianne furrows her brow, glancing from him to me, then back again. The only person in the room who looks more confused and stunned is Westbrook's girlfriend.

"Thank you, Mr. Westbrook," Marianne finally manages. "I just need your signature on a few additional documents and we're done here."

I lunge for Westbrook, grab him by his overpriced shirt and throw him to the floor. I pummel him, gleefully slamming my fists into his face as he cries and begs me to stop. As he curls into the fetal position in an attempt to protect himself, I kick at him, blasting the point of my shoe into his ribs and back. He grunts and tries to crawl away, but I'm on him, choking him from behind and pulling him closer so I can sink my teeth into the side of his neck. Ripping and tearing a chunk of flesh free in a bloody spray, I spit it out on the kitchen floor, then throw him forward onto his belly. While he weeps and pees all over himself, I find a wooden block storing knives on the counter, slide free the largest blade in the bunch, then turn him over so I can slit his stomach open and yank free everything inside. I want to feel his wet organs squish and pulsate in my bare hands, I want to feel his warm blood flow and drip between my fingers, I want to taste it and wear it on my skin. I want to show him his own guts, to hold them up to his face as he wails in agony and horror at his own vivisection and—

"Stop," Westbrook says.

The sound of his voice snaps me out of my dream—or whatever it was—and I see that he has now moved farther away from me. His back to the refrigerator and his face tangled into a scowl of terror and confusion, he reaches into his shirt and pulls free a small gold cross he wears on a chain around his neck. His fingers slowly stroke it as he stares at me with horror, like everything that played across my mind's eye played across his as well. He's seen Hell. And I've shown it to him.

"Christ Jesus," Westbrook mutters.

"You really think He hears your prayers?" I say evenly. "He doesn't."

Trembling and nearly in tears, he whispers, "What the hell are you?"

The desire for violence recedes and I can feel my body relaxing, my mind returning to me. "Just a public servant a few IQ points away from being a meter maid," I answer with a faux smile, "remember?"

"Mr. Westbrook," Marianne says through obvious confusion, "are you all right?"

He slowly shakes his head. "No. No, I—I don't think I am."

I turn back to the woman in the Capri pants. "If you stay with this man, eventually he'll either cripple you or kill you. You don't need to be degraded and abused like this, and whatever he tells you, what he's done and will do to you has nothing to do with love. Ms. Feeney's going to leave you her business card. If you need her, let her know and she can get you help or get you away from this piece of shit, okay?"

Pale as a ghost, the woman nods but says nothing.

Marianne stands there frozen, mouth hanging open. "I'll be in the car," I tell her, and then looking back over my shoulder at Westbrook, add, "Be a good boy, sign your papers and forget about the rest of this. Or I'll have to come back for another visit."

Westbrook nods rapidly, still clutching his cross.

Outside, I stand on the steps, light a cigarette and smoke it in the rain. The rain is cooling and sobering, and like coming down from a drug high, I slowly return to...to what? Normal? I'm not even sure what that is anymore.

A car glides down the street, rolling slowly past the brownstone. A boxy sedan, the windows are tinted black and don't allow me to see inside, but my reaction to the car is instinctual, primal. Whoever is inside that sedan is there for me.

At the corner the car stops...waits...then turns, vanishing into the rain.

It has no license plate.

Just as I take my final drag and flick the cigarette away, Marianne emerges from the brownstone door behind me. Without a word, she pushes by me and stomps awkwardly down the steps to the street.

"Marianne—"

"Just get in the fucking car," she says without stopping.

I follow her down the steps and back into her Mazda. The minute we're inside she turns the heater on low, and I realize how cold the rain has become. I wipe water from my eyes and wait as Marianne, seething, stares straight ahead at nothing. As she struggles to put her anger into words, her chest rises and falls with a rapid cadence, and her normally pale complexion is flushed bright red.

Finally, she turns to me, her emerald eyes ablaze but her tone surprisingly soft and calm. "Cam, are you out of your mind?"

"It's a distinct possibility."

"You think this is funny?"

"No, I don't think it's funny at all."

She shakes her head as if hoping to dislodge something. "Why did you do that? Why did you even come in? Why would you risk my job like that? We're talking about my job, Cam, my livelihood. If you want to ruin yours, that's your business, but why would you try to destroy mine along with it?"

"Westbrook won't do anything, trust me. He won't say a word to anyone."

"How did you frighten him like that? What did you do?"

"Nothing, he's garbage, don't worry about it."

"*Don't worry about it?*" She laughs involuntarily. "What's gotten into you?"

Something…evil…

"I'm not sure," I tell her.

"It's like you're an entirely different person. The Cam Horne I know, the Cam Horne who trained me—the right way, by the book—the Cam Horne I worked with for years, would never dream of behaving the way you just did in there. And since when do you *smoke?*" Through gritted teeth she continues. "I know you realize what Westbrook could do. If he files a complaint—and he has a witness—we're both fucked. I can't even count the number of laws you just broke. It's going to be *both* our asses, Cam, not just yours. Do you just not give a shit, or what?"

"He won't do anything."

"How do you know? You can't be sure of that."

"Yes I can, and I am."

She pinches the bridge of her nose, up near her eyes, and sighs. "I guess I thought we were more than coworkers," she says softly. "I thought we were friends."

"We are friends."

"No," she says, snapping her head up straight. "No, because a friend would not do what you just did to me. A friend wouldn't risk another friend's job."

I want to touch her just then. I want to take her hands in mine and tell her to look me in the eye so I can assure her everything will be all right and that I care about her very deeply. But I don't know what she'll see if she does look closer, and the last thing I want to do is hurt or upset her more than I already have. "I'm sorry, but—"

"Sorry isn't gonna cut it this time," she says.

"Nothing will happen. Just stay quiet about this and—"

"*Really*, ya think? Actually, I was planning to run right back to Roz and fill her in."

We're quiet for awhile. Rain batters the car. The world outside seems a million miles away. I'm cold and wet and it feels like thousands of insects are scurrying about beneath my skin, trying to burrow out through the pores.

"I need to see Copeland's file," I tell her.

"Why? Are you planning to go threaten him too? Not a chance."

"I need that file."

"Go home, Cam. Get to a doctor."

"Marianne, I—"

"Get out of my car."

"Just let me use your laptop for two seconds and I'll go."

"I swear to *God* I will call 911," she snaps. "Get out of my car."

Something moves deep inside me…slithering…

"Please," I say, just above a whisper. "Let me see the file and I'll go. *Please.*"

Don't make me hurt you.

"I can't trust your judgment. You're too much of a wild card at this point."

"I already know his address, if this was about going there and doing something to him, I would've already done it. I don't need the file for that."

"Then why *do* you need it?"

"I want to go over his background again so I have a better idea of who I'm dealing with, all right? There's something about this guy, Marianne, something that doesn't add up and I…look, there's no way my looking at it again can be tied back to you. I was never here, this never happened."

Please don't make me take the laptop from you.

Marianne's beautiful eyes, so sad and angry all at once, lock onto mine and hold. But this time, rather than terror, all I see is pity. And it breaks my heart.

Several seconds live and die before she reaches into her satchel, turns on the laptop, enters her password and hands me the computer.

"Hurry up," she says. "And this never happened either."

CHAPTER EIGHT

The light through the trees…the most beautiful light I've ever seen, it filters through the leaves and branches, washing down and falling across me like a blanket gently dropped from above. Lying on my back on the forest floor, limbs spread out like a snow angel, I look up at those trees—silent giants gathered above me—and feel so insignificant. Yet I am part of them somehow. We are connected. We are brethren. The forest, the earth, the bed of pine needles, the insects and animals, the wink of vast sky peeking through the canopy of treetop branches and leaves, all of it flows through me like lifeblood. And I flow through it. We are one, a circle, a snake eating its own tail. I breathe deeply and smell the forest as the golden sunlight warms my face.

And in that wonderful moment, I see it all there before me, so close I could reach out and grab it if only I had the courage. Unfolding like a magnificent dream, such overwhelming beauty makes me want to cry tears not of rage, terror or even sorrow, but extraordinary joy.

I remember it all.

But most of all, I remember that beautiful light bleeding through the trees.

* * *

The trendy coffee shop four blocks over is bustling, so Marianne and I choose a table near the back we hope might provide at least a modicum of privacy and settle in, she with some sort of triple-latte-whipped-cream-something-or-other, and me with a blasphemous cup of standard black coffee.

Everything and everyone moves around me like ants. It all makes me even more uncomfortable, the people inside and the cars outside, the walkers drifting by windows distorted with rain, the whispers at the very outskirts of my mind. I sip coffee and run a hand over my face, across the stubble on my cheeks and chin. Marianne sits across from me, and I can tell she's trying desperately to make sense of me and to think of something—anything—to say that might make this situation more tenable.

Copeland's file revealed nothing prior to 2005, and subsequent searches on our database as well as general searches came up empty.

"Do you understand now why I wanted to see the rest of Copeland's file?" I ask, voice gravelly and my throat feeling as if I've spent the last hour screaming at the top of my lungs.

"Honestly, no."

"Because there isn't anything else, the rest of his file is empty."

"We don't have full histories on all registrants, Cam," Marianne reminds me. "In fact, we have them on very few."

"But there's some indication and proof of their existence. You saw the file same as me, you saw the other searches I did. There's literally nothing on Copeland prior."

Marianne holds her coffee in both hands, gazing down into it as if enthralled. "It's not like there's no trace of him at all."

"Yes, it is like that. There isn't a trace of him before that. He appears in 2005. Prior to that there's nothing, Marianne, *nothing*."

I can tell from the look on her face she doesn't want to acknowledge this. She feels the need to chalk it up to errors or coincidence, because doing anything but will require further critical thought and—God forbid—perhaps even action, and she wants no part of that. I can't blame her necessarily, but I can't go along with it either.

"Okay, so let's cut right to it. What are you suggesting, Cam?"

"Pretty obvious, isn't it? It's as if he didn't exist prior to 2005."

She looks up from her coffee, an eyebrow arched. "Well, that's totally possible so that must be it. He was hatched on a rock in Rhode Island in the summer of 2005 and crawled out of his shell a thirty-five-year-old man. Then he committed his crimes, went to prison, got out and moved to Mass. Definitely, makes perfect sense." She sips her coffee. "Christ Almighty."

"Then explain it."

"Explain what?"

"There is literally no information on him prior to 2005."

"No, you just haven't come across any you want to consider. We have his date of birth, his place of birth, the schools he attended, his previous addresses and the jobs he held. Those are all things that prove his existence, and they can be—and in some cases I'm sure they have been—verified. As if such a thing needs to be proven. I'll tell you, I've had some ridiculous-ass conversations in my life, but this one takes the cake."

"His previous addresses and the jobs he held do not go back further than 2005, that's what I'm trying to tell you. We have a date of birth and a place of birth, and some high school he allegedly attended. But those are just forms, Marianne, documents. They can be forged. There's nothing to back any of that up, no corroborating proof that any of it is true."

"There's nothing to indicate those things have been forged either."

"Where's the rest of his information? If he'd worked or lived somewhere during those years, there'd be evidence of it, records. There isn't."

Marianne waves at the air between us the way one shoos away a flying bug. "Are you honestly sitting here suggesting Alfred Copeland didn't *exist* until 2005? Because if that's what you're suggesting, then I'm driving you to the nearest hospital right now, and I mean right-fucking-now."

"There's something going on," I tell her.

She looks away. After a moment she seems to collect herself and says, "Cam, I've always looked up to you, and I have nothing but the utmost respect for you. I hope you know that. You trained me, you gave me my shot. If it weren't for you, I wouldn't have this gig or any of the successes I've had in the position since, and I appreciate that, I really do. I'll always be grateful to you for taking me under your wing and helping me."

Here it comes.

"But you need help. You *have* to get help, do you understand?"

I nod, embarrassed and angry all at once. "Sure."

Marianne reaches across the table and places her hand on mine. "It'll be okay."

And then something occurs to me. "Who has his file now?"

"Roz divided your caseload between all of us."

"Who got Copeland's?"

"I did." Her hand slowly slides away. "Roz gave it to me."

"Why didn't you tell me?"

"What difference does it make?"

I watch this woman I've known for so long, worked with so closely, and wonder if I really know her at all. "Look into his past beyond 2005."

"Why would I do that?" she asks. "I have all the relevant information on Copeland I need in his file."

"Because I'm asking you to," I say evenly. "Half the members of your family are cops. Call in a favor, ask them to run him and look as deep as they can. Tell them you want everything and anything they can find on him."

Marianne puts her coffee aside and pulls her raincoat back on over her shoulders like a shawl. "If I do that—and that's a big *if*—what exactly would I be looking for?"

"Anything that proves he was alive before 2005."

"Of course he was alive before 2005. He's forty-three years old. He's been alive since 1970, do the math."

"Find me the evidence," I tell her. "But stay away from him."

"There's no need to see him at this point. I'll probably do a follow-up to your visit in a couple weeks just to make sure he's complying with everything, but—"

"No," I say, lunging and grabbing hold of her wrist before I even realize what I've done. "Stay away from him. He's—"

"Let go," she says, pulling at my fingers with her free hand. "Cam, *let go.*"

I do.

"What the hell?" she says, rubbing her wrist. "That hurt, asshole."

"I'm sorry. I didn't mean to hurt you. I wouldn't—"

"Really?" She stands and moves back, as if to be sure she's beyond my reach. "Little late for that."

"Marianne, I—"

"I'll see what I can find out about Copeland's past, all right? If I find anything worth reporting, I'll be in touch. Either way, don't call me, I'll call you. Got it?"

I want to tell her I can see blood pouring from her eyes. I can hear her screams and pleas for mercy. I want to tell her I can feel her agony and fear and see what awaits her if she isn't careful around Copeland and the evil moving all around her. But instead I simply say, "Yes."

Then she turns and is gone, another lost soul in the wind and rain, one more sheep with her head bowed and eyes closed, moving quietly to slaughter.

* * *

Time is broken.

My parents are dead, and I miss them dearly. Not a day goes by that I don't think of them at least once or twice, and even in all this madness—perhaps because of it—they come to me while I drive home, their faces watching from the shadows of other worlds. Sad and beautiful and so very far away, they remain a part of me.

The windshield wipers squeal against glass, reminding me the rain has stopped. As I switch them off, I remember my mother. A quiet and dignified woman, she worked for the post office, enjoyed classical music, and was a voracious reader. Nearly all my memories of my mother involve reading material, as she always seemed to be carrying a book or a magazine of some sort. I remember being very young and playing on the floor in our den while she sat in the rocking chair by the window, reading one of her books. I can almost see her slowly rocking in that chair, the sun coming through the windows and framing her in an orange glow. I'd often gaze up at her and marvel at how beautiful she was, but we'd sometimes go hours without speaking. Neither of us minded. I knew she was there, near me, with me, and she knew the same about me. And that was enough.

As I exit the highway and head for home, my father comes to me.

With a mischievous grin and a bellowing laugh that was nothing short of contagious, he was a jovial and gentle man; a salesman who worked hard his entire life but never complained or made excuses. If there was a bright side, my father found it, and if there wasn't, he created one. He was a good provider, a loving husband and an attentive father. Much like my mother, he excelled at nearly everything he touched, and while his musical tastes ran more toward Frank Sinatra, Judy Garland and Dean Martin than my mother's classical, and he rarely read anything other than the sports page in the local newspaper, he and my mother were perfectly suited to each other.

When I got older, I realized how deeply my parents were in love with each other, even after decades of marriage. Their love never went stale, never got old. But they did, and soon the vibrant people they'd once been were gone.

I'm an only child, and while I sometimes wish I'd had siblings, looking back I see how fortunate I was to have such loving and kind parents all to myself. So many kids I knew had issues with their parents, or had a mother or father with serious issues, but not me. I was blessed. We weren't rich and didn't have the best of everything, as some of the wealthier families on the other side of town did, but we had love. Real love, the way it's supposed to be. We were a family.

How I miss that. How I miss them. How I miss *us*.

Although it is still early afternoon, the previous rains have left the day much darker than usual. The sky is smeared with gray and a light wind has arrived. Finally home, I pull onto our road and drive slowly toward the house. Once in the driveway, I step from the car. Still dazed and clinging to my memories, I watch a sudden gust of wind knock leaves from a nearby tree. They spiral gracefully to the ground, joining others in a small pile near the base of the tree.

Our house is dark and quiet, and there is no sign of anyone in the backyard, but behind the curtained windows of my neighbor Bruce Deacon's house, lights burn dimly. Bruce is home. But then, Bruce is always home.

Before I can make it to the door, I see him coming around the side of the house pulling a large trash barrel behind him. "Cam-o," he says, offering an apathetic wave with his free hand. Only Bruce calls me *Cam-o*, and while I've never cared for it, there's certainly no harm intended, so I always let it go.

"Hey, Bruce," I reply, "how's life?"

He gets the barrel to the end of the driveway, then rests his hands on his waist. "Taking a lot longer than I thought," he sighs. "What are you doing home this time of day?"

"Taking a few days off," I tell him.

In wrinkled khakis, a faded golf shirt and a fishing hat that looks as if someone has quickly slapped it on his head without his knowledge, Bruce initially exudes a crotchety old grandfather vibe, but a closer look reveals desperation and heartbreak, a man who has given up and no longer makes an effort to conceal that fact. "Vacation, huh?" he says. "Got time for a beer then?"

I hesitate, look to his house, then my own. Something is standing at our bedroom window looking down at me, but just as this registers in my mind, it steps from view, a black humanoid smudge darting across already dark glass. A tremor grabs hold of me and I shuffle my feet in an attempt to disguise it. "Okay, yeah," I tell Bruce. "Sure, I'll have a beer, why not?"

He leads me up the narrow stone walk to his front door. A wreath his late wife Margaret hung on it three years ago, the last Christmas she was alive, is still suspended from a nail on the door, long since turned brown, the once bright red satin ribbon at its center tattered, stained and faded to more of a light pink color.

"That was a hell of a rain, wasn't it?" Bruce says, pushing through the door and moving up the stairs that greet us.

"Yeah," I say absently, closing the door behind me and following him up the stairs. "It was really coming down."

"Like a pony pissing on a flat rock," he adds.

A musty smell mixed with the aroma of fried foods, cigars and body odor hangs in the air, and the place is a mess. Straight ahead, a kitchen awaits us, to the left his living room and to the right a hallway leading to the bedrooms. Margaret has been gone a little over two years now, but the house looks exactly as it did when she was alive, only horribly unkempt and neglected.

It's been so long since he cared, Bruce seems not to notice.

I try to remember the last time I was in his home, but can't. It's been a while, several months—maybe even a year—and though the place looked similar, it's gotten worse. I can't imagine how he lives like this, in such self-imposed squalor.

"At least it beats snow," he says. "Don't have to shovel it."

I throw back the obligatory, "True."

As he goes to the refrigerator to grab a couple beers, I drift into the living room but remain standing. The wall-to-wall carpet is filthy, pitted with burn holes and covered with debris and trash. The couch is covered with old newspapers and dirty clothes, and a badly worn recliner is empty but surrounded by beer bottles. A freestanding ashtray is perched next to it, overflowed with cigar butts, ash and discarded stick matches. On a rack against the back wall are an old tube television and a vcr. The walls are decorated with cheap art and photographs of him and Margaret. In most, Bruce is decked out in his full fireman's regalia, and it's hard to imagine that the virile and heroic firefighter pictured is the same person.

"It's cheap shit but gets the job done," he says, joining me in the living room and handing me a can of beer.

I glance at the label. It's a brand I've never heard of. "Thanks."

"Take a seat." He pushes some newspapers from one section of couch onto the floor, then goes to his recliner and gracelessly flops down onto it with a grunt. "How's the wife doing?"

"Good. She's good." I sit on the edge of the couch and try not to notice all the clutter and filth. A photograph of Margaret hung over the fireplace smiles down at me, and I remember when she was alive and what a sweet woman she was.

Bruce gives a quick nod and takes a pull on his beer. "You're one lucky sonofabitch, Cam-o, one lucky son of a bitch. Remy's a good woman, and a good woman is hard to find."

"I'm sure most women would argue it's even harder to find a good man," I say in as pleasant a tone as I can muster.

He flashes me one of his cranky looks. "Yeah, except that women are crazy."

"All of them?"

"Every last one, it's just a matter of degrees. Some are crazier than others. The key is to find one that's not too crazy, one you can live with and love and who'll love you without driving you crazy too or putting you in an early grave." He looks to one of the photos of his deceased wife and raises his beer can. "Like my Margie. Now *that* was a good woman."

"That she was, Bruce." I can't even imagine outliving Remy, and my heart breaks for the old man when I think about what he's been through.

"Cherish every minute you've got with her," he tells me, "every second."

"I try to."

"Don't try, do it." He takes a long drink of beer, then belches under his breath. "How the hell did two scrubs like us ever land such good women?" He chuckles but there's no joy in it, no real humor, just more pain.

I smile awkwardly and take a quick sip of beer so I don't have to respond.

"Yeah…so anyway," Bruce says through a sigh, "looks like the

Bruins are going to have a good team this year, huh?"

"I haven't been following the off-season stuff very closely, been so busy."

"Got any interesting cases going at work?"

Bruce asks me this a lot, and I always have to give him the same answer. "I'm not really allowed to get into the particulars, sorry. I've been busy though."

"Figures, with all the creeps and weirdoes walking the streets these days," he says, shaking his head. "I'll never know how you deal with that scum all day long."

"I wonder that a lot myself."

"Hell, I remember when I was just a kid coming out of school. I thought about being a cop, but I just didn't have the right temperament for police work. Figured I'd wind up breaking my foot off in somebody's ass, so I decided to go fight fires instead. That was before I really knew anything about the enemy, though."

"The enemy?"

"Fire," he says with a smile that seems genuine but evaporates in seconds. Still, whenever Bruce talks about his time as a fireman, he becomes more coherent and eloquent, as if some dormant section of his alcohol-soaked brain temporarily comes to life whenever he broaches the subject. "In my job I had to become intimately familiar with it, had to get to know fire and understand it as the enemy it was. The mistake most people make is that they underestimate it and treat it like an inanimate object. What they don't realize is...fire's *alive*."

Flashes of flames fill my head, engulfing countless screaming and bloody souls, their bulging eyes and scorched faces and bodies melting like wax.

"It's a living thing," Bruce continues. "And it's a predator. Anything in its path is prey to be devoured. It has no remorse, no regret and no fear, and it'll never stop unless someone or something kills it. It's a perfect organism is what it is, a perfect killing machine."

I drink more beer and the hellish visions fade.

"Thing is, it's a sneaky son of a bitch too. Sometimes you think it's dead and gone, but it isn't. It's just hiding, waiting for a better opportunity to strike, and just because you can't see it or feel it or even smell it, doesn't mean it's not there. It can be inches away from you and you'll never even know it. By the time you do, it's too late. It wins." He finishes his beer and drops the can to the floor with the others. "Once you've been in the fire—I mean really in it, surrounded by a burning sea of it—you never forget it, I can tell you that, Cam-o. You know its power, you feel it, because you're in its midst. And you realize it's there to kill you. It *wants* to kill you. So you either lay down and let it take your sorry ass, or fight and claw your way out. Either way, the fire's there for one purpose and one purpose only, to consume you and everything else in its way."

I look to him, wanting to know what he knows.

"I've seen the power of fire, been deep in the flames, lost friends to it. Came to know fire, and it came to know me. I'd say, after all those years in the department, me and fire can go ahead and call it a push, at least for now." He struggles up to his feet. "That's why I don't fear Hell."

"I don't believe in Hell," I tell him, though I'm not so sure anymore.

"Hell doesn't want you to believe in it," Bruce says, shuffling off to the kitchen for more beer. "And fire? Shit, it's counting on it."

I try to picture this frail and drunken old man breaking down doors with an ax and rushing into burning buildings, saving kittens and children and families trapped in the flames. None of it makes any sense. Bruce looks like he couldn't lift an ax or run down a city block if his life depended on it. But there was a time when he could do those things, when he was young and heroic and strong. Time robbed him of it all, just as it will one day rob us all.

Not you...

Will there come a day when Remy and I are old and cling to each other like frightened children, hanging on to whatever scraps of life—of us—remain?

You will never be old…You have never been young…

But I was young once. I was a happy child with loving parents and a good home.

Lies…all of it, lies…

Bullshit.

Before I realize what I've done, I crush the empty beer can in my hand. It makes a horrible sound as it implodes.

"You crushed that thing like it said something about your mother," Bruce cracks as he returns from the kitchen with two fresh beers.

"Sorry."

"Like I give a shit," he says, thrusting a new can at me. As I take it, he plucks the crushed one from my hand and tosses it over his shoulder. "Look around, son, the ship sailed on me giving a damn about much of anything a long time ago. Running a bunch of cans over to the redemption center isn't exactly a priority these days."

I give a halfhearted smile just so he'll know I get it. "Can I ask you a question?"

Bruce returns to his recliner, and once there, pops opens his beer and takes a few gulps. "Free country, Cam-o. Well, used to be anyway."

I open my beer. "Have you heard that car alarm going off every morning?"

He looks at me, bleary-eyed, but says nothing.

"Off that way," I say, pointing with my beer can toward the back of the house. "On the other side of the woods behind the house, it's been going off every morning, waking me up. Have you heard it?"

"Nah," he finally answers.

I don't believe him. My eyes look to the kitchen and down the dark hallway adjacent the living room. Suddenly, I'm not so sure we're alone here. Maybe we never were. "It's been happening for days," I tell him.

"I don't go in those woods," Bruce says, downing more beer, racing to become even drunker than he already is. "Don't like them, something creepy about those trees out there. I got no reason to go out there, so I don't. Some places, just like some people, you just need to stay clear of, know what I mean?"

"No, what do you mean?"

He fidgets in the recliner like a kid. He knows something. I can feel it, and if I listen closely enough, I can hear those terrible distant voices telling me so, whispering his secrets to me. But rather than speaking English, they're whispering in another language I can't identify and don't understand, something ancient that brings forth even stranger visions into my head. Sands…deserts…blood…wooden crosses decorating the landscape, men nailed to them in the burning sun…their cries for mercy hidden in the winds of time.

"What's wrong with those woods?" I ask.

"I don't know," he whines, sipping more beer. "I'm just a lonely old man."

Hurt him. Make him tell you. Snap something on the old fuck.

I take another drink. "What's back there, Bruce?"

"How the hell should I know? Nothing, I'm just talking. Those woods make me uncomfortable. Don't things make you uncomfortable sometimes? Not trying to make a federal case out of it." He finishes his beer and throws it aside. "For Christ's sake, I shouldn't have to take this kind of shit in my own place, not—not in my own place. I know it's a shithole but it's all I got, okay? I invited you up here to shoot the shit and kill a few beers, that's all, like a good neighbor should, right? Like I'm *supposed* to, I—I'm doing my part."

"Your part?" I finish my beer, throw it at the floor with the others and rise to my feet. He's frightened suddenly, but by far more than me. "What's going on, Bruce?"

He puts his hands up like the victim of a robbery. "I don't know."

The fucker's lying to you. Teach him a lesson.

"You've heard that alarm just like I have, haven't you."

It wasn't a question but he answers anyway. "Yeah, okay? I have, I—I hear it but it's none of my business so I don't pay any attention."

Make him tell you the truth.

"Have you seen the young guy in my yard?" I press, stepping closer to him. "Sitting out by the fire pit, have you seen him?"

"Yeah," he says softly.

Can you smell that? It's fear.

"Who is he?"

"Fuck if I know, he's your friend, isn't he?"

Can you hear his blood moving through him? Can you taste it?

"What does he want with me?" My hands tighten to fists. "What's happening to me, Bruce?"

"I don't know, I—I'm trying to tell you I don't know."

Rip the pathetic old fuck apart.

I move closer. "I can make you tell me."

"Tell you what," he says, scooting toward the edge of the recliner, "I'll get us another couple beers and we'll forget all about this and have some laughs, okay?"

Hurt him, Zeke. Hurt him.

Zeke…Shelly called me by that name and I'd chalked it up to her drunken state. But now…

"Who's Zeke?" I ask him.

Bruce squints, as if he's losing sight of me. "Zeke?"

"My name is Cameron Horne!"

He nods helplessly. "Yeah, I…I know, Cam-o."

Kill him, Zeke. Beat him to death with your bare hands.

"You're going to tell me what I need to know."

He stares at me, feigning confusion.

I lunge, grab hold of him by the front of his golf shirt and yank him to his feet. He is surprisingly light as I shake him like a rag doll. "Tell me, you fuck! Tell me or I swear to God I'll kill you!"

"Cam-o, I—Christ—I don't know what you want me to tell you!"

I backhand him across the mouth. He cries out as his head snaps to the side and his fishing hat slides off to reveal his bald, liver-spotted head. "What's happening to me? Tell me what's happening to me!"

"I don't know, I—I'm just trying to be your friend, I—please, I don't know what you want." He begins to cry and his body goes limp in my hands, his head bowed as tears stream his flushed face. "Margie, help me, I—I don't know what to do, I—I didn't do anything, I just want my Margie, I—please, I…"

What have I done? Christ Almighty, what the hell have I done?

"Bruce, I…" I place him back in the recliner as gently as I can. "I'm sorry. I—I'm so sorry. Are you all right?"

He slumps over, weeping openly. "Do it. Kill me. Put me out of my misery. I miss my Margie. I don't want to be here anymore, I want to go home. I want to go home to my Margie. Don't make me stay here. I want to go home."

I place a hand flat on Bruce's back and rub it. Overwhelmed with grief and guilt, I try to think of something to say, some way to comfort him. But there's nothing I can do. I can't make this right and we both know it. "Take it easy," I say anyway. "It's going to be all right. I'm so sorry. I…please forgive me, I don't know what the hell's wrong with me, I…please…"

The old man cries, his face buried in his hands and his body bucking as he sobs.

I back away, trembling and overcome with guilt.

Slowly, Bruce raises his head from his hands and looks at me. "I could die tonight and this world wouldn't miss a beat. It'd be like I was never even here."

"You said that before," I tell him.

"There is no before."

"I don't understand."

"I know." He nods, his face a combination of torment and sorrow. "Me either."

CHAPTER NINE

After the rain, the world smells like wet leaves. I stand in the backyard watching the woods, staring at the trees and the darkness between them, seeing nothing but knowing there is more there than I realize or understand. Something is looking back, I'm sure of it. Part of me wants to leave the self-imposed boundary of my yard and walk into these woods, but I can't bring myself to do it. My feet remain anchored to the moist ground, as somewhere behind me, in his lonely slipshod house, poor Bruce Deacon sits, a helpless pile of wrinkled flesh and decaying bone, weeping for a past he will never again possess, a present that eludes him like whispers and a future he will never know.

Now I know he weeps for us both.

Afraid to explore the woods but hesitant to go in the house, I look back over my shoulder at the deck and sliders and watch for signs of intruders or dark blotches moving by the windows.

There is nothing but an empty house. Was there ever anything more? Does it matter? Does it really make a difference at this point?

I cross the yard to the deck, unlock the sliders and slip inside stealthily, a thief burglarizing my own home.

The house is cemetery-quiet, the rooms empty. I am alone.

Standing in the kitchen over the sink, I light a cigarette and smoke it in silence.

Mind and heart racing, hands shaking, I try to decide what to do next. Maybe rather than waiting to hear from work I should make my confession to Remy, tell her what's been happening and check myself in somewhere before…

Before what, I hurt someone else or maybe even myself? Before what's left of my mind shuts down or shatters and renders me one of those lost and forgotten souls locked away in some dingy institution babbling about devils and hellfire? Before—

Before we come for you…

I flick my cigarette into the sink, run the water, then move toward the great room, approaching it with caution, as if negotiating a dark alley rather than the familiar vicinity of my home. But it really isn't my home anymore, is it? Whatever is stalking me—be it insanity or something else—it's taken it, stolen it from me, if not literally, then certainly in the sense that it no longer represents the comfort and safety it should, the personal sanctuary from an often mad world it once was.

At the bar, I pour myself a drink and scan the photographs on the wall. Everyone I've ever loved and cared about looks back, imprisoned in frames and frozen in time beneath glass.

Lies…

"Shut up," I growl, my eyes scanning the walls, the ceiling, the corners. "Shut the fuck up."

Use that anger, embrace it—

"Shut up, goddamn you!"

I power the drink down like a shot, feel it burn through me as I rub my temples and assure myself these voices are my own. I'm making them happen, they're my creations, and if I created them, then I can destroy them as well, I can control them, re-strain and cage them like the dangerous and unpredictable feral animals they are.

We're here for you, Zeke.

"Stop calling me that!" I slam a fist down onto the bar, rat-tling the glasses on the shelves inside.

We're here to help you, Zeke.

"My name is Cameron Horne," I say, pacing about furiously, a tiger walking his cage. "I know who I am. I know who I am!"

We know who you are, too.

"I'm Cameron Horne." I return to the bar, pour myself an-other drink. "Cam—Cameron Horne, that's who I am."

It's almost time, Zeke.

I swallow it down, then push away from the bar with such force I stagger back and nearly lose my balance. "I'm sick. I— I'm sick, this isn't real."

The phone rings, startling me.

I grab the cordless from its cradle on an end table.

The ID reads: UNKNOWN CALLER. I punch the answer button, and gripping the phone tight, raise it to my ear. "Hello?"

Although no one answers, I can hear the faint sound of measured breath, slow and steady…or is it…wind? An ancient wind from another place, another time…

"Hello?" I say again.

The last thing I remember is a blinding flash of light and a high-pitched screech that feels as if it's tearing through my skull and piercing my brain.

* * *

It raced through the wires, raw energy—impulse and conscious-ness in one—alive and firing, employing the same door it entered through to make its escape. Using the wires as a pathway, it charged on, spiraling into the ether, surging through time and matter like a stone skipping across the smooth surface of a pond. A predator un-seen, it bled into the atmosphere, dragging its kill to immeasurable darkness just beyond the sky, the reaches of reason and the somber face of God. Oblivion, it wanted nothing less, a kingdom of fire where trophies kneel before altars of blood and bone like the lapdogs they were.

* * *

Lights crash and explode all around me. Headlights blur and glare through the darkness beyond the windshield, the horrible screeching silenced, swallowed by my own sudden, gasping intake of breath.

"What is it?" Remy asks from behind the wheel.

I don't answer until I realize I'm in the car, the front passenger seat, and that the lights belong to a truck passing us from the opposite direction. I bring a hand to my face, run it across my mouth, wipe it free of spittle and give my wife a sideways glance.

"Did you fall asleep?" Remy presses, smiling at me awkwardly, her face bathed in the eerie green glow of dashboard light.

How the hell did I get here?

"Yeah, I…I must've dozed off," I say.

We cruise down a quaint, tree-lined suburban street, the headlights illuminating the sidewalks and portions of neatly trimmed yards and shrubbery. The homes on either side of us— most much nicer than our own—sit in darkness but for an occasional porch lamp or light-filled window. I recognize the neighborhood. We're still in town but a good ten to fifteen minutes from the house.

I search my mind for memories but all I can remember is answering the phone and hearing that horrible shriek. At some point since then I have changed into a fresh pair of khakis, a casual sports coat and a pair a loafers. I can smell aftershave on my neck, so I touch my face. I am clean shaven, and my mouth is fresh and clean, my teeth having apparently been brushed fairly recently.

"Are you feeling any better?" Remy slows the car and makes a left.

"Not really," I tell her. "I'm so…*tired.*"

We pull into the paved driveway alongside an older but meticulously maintained saltbox clapboard house. Remy turns off the engine, turns to me and takes my hand in hers. "We don't have to stay long. Let's just make an appearance so there won't be any hard feelings, then we'll go, okay?"

I want to tell her to start the car and get us out of here. The world is crumbling all around me and she expects me to attend some ridiculous cocktail party? But the optimistic look on her beautiful face stops me. She wants—needs—so badly for me to be there for her, to come through, to take part in things like this that are important to her, and I'd rather die than disappoint or hurt her. She saved my life, gave me happiness I never knew was even possible, and despite all my shortcomings and struggles, Remy always believes in me, even when I don't deserve it, and has always had my back. How can I let her down? How can I break down and confess my sins to her, tell her I have no memory of how I got here and that I'm so scared I can barely think or breathe or—

"Sweetie, if you're seriously not up for this, we can leave now," she says, her expression shifting to deep concern as she caresses my shoulder. "You look...off."

"I'm okay, just not feeling terribly sociable."

"No," she says, considering me the way I imagine she considers her students at school when she suspects she's not being told the truth. "There's something more, I can feel it. You haven't been acting like yourself for awhile now. What's the matter? You can tell me, it'll be all right."

I take her hands in mine again, kiss them and press them against my cheek. It feels wonderful. It feels...*safe*. "Do you know how much I love you?"

"Aw, *Cam*," she says, her face flushing. "Of course I do, and I love you too, sweetie, more than anything in the world."

I clear my throat and steel myself. "Promise we won't stay long?"

A smile slowly surfaces. "Cross my heart."

I look to the house. Unlike the others on the street it is lit up and welcoming, and through the light-filled windows I can see a few people milling about, chatting, holding drinks and nibbling hors d'oeuvres.

"All right then," I tell her. "Come on."

* * *

"Well, look," Dario says, swirling the red wine around in his glass and holding it up to the light as if he's never seen it before, "Charles Baudelaire maintained that literature and evil are inseparable."

Remy and I stand listening, along with two other teachers from her school, Jeffrey Stanton and Isabella Costa.

Jeffrey chuckles. "Baudelaire's full of shit."

"That seems a bit harsh," Isabella says.

"But it's true. Talk about drawing parallels where none need exist. The thought process that allows one to arrive at his conclusion is so infantile it's breathtaking." Jeffrey sips his drink and looks to Remy and me for support. "Jump in at any time."

I shrug awkwardly. A bunch of high school teachers sitting around pretending to be college professors, and pretentious ones at that, I can't imagine why I loathe socializing with these people. Dario's real name is Darren, but he changed it because he felt his birth name wasn't exotic enough and therefore didn't properly convey who he truly was. His wife Sue, an unassuming and pencil-thin mousey brunette with a penchant for cardigan sweaters and long skirts, is equally irritating, but mostly due to her misguided worship of her husband. I often wonder what someone like Remy sees in them, colleagues or not. "Sorry," I say, "this is a bit outside my wheelhouse."

"You claim it's an infantile stance," Dario says before Remy can respond, ignoring me completely, "but Baudelaire himself said on several occasions that there were many childish aspects to literature and evil—so he admits this—he just refuses to condemn either, and to me, not only is that bolder, it's infinitely more interesting."

"But he also blames the writer for penning anything that could be perceived as having a dark—or *evil*, as he describes it—theme," Jeffrey counters. "Which, come on, is nothing short of preposterous."

"Hold on," Dario says, adjusting his position on the arm of the couch but remaining seated. With his tweed jacket, grandiose gestures and mop of salt-and-pepper curly hair, he reminds me of a host from some local PBS pledge drive. "He also admits that it's exactly that kind of theme that makes the writing interesting."

Jeffrey, a tall and gangly sort, balding but with a full beard, responds, "Yes, while holding the writer culpable for what's being written."

"Are you suggesting artists have no culpability whatsoever?"

"It depends on the work, but generally, no, I don't think they—"

"For God's sake, Dario," Isabella jumps in, "much as I think calling Baudelaire full of shit is too harsh, he was of the belief that writing wasn't real work and that writers were evil because they didn't hold real jobs. What sort of archaic nonsense is that?"

Dario waves at her with his free hand, as if swatting away an insect. "You're oversimplifying his stance."

"Is that even possible?" Jeffrey barks with laughter while Isabella, his girlfriend, gives him a conspiratorial pat on the shoulder.

Remy, still having not gotten a word in, looks at me and winks.

I smile vaguely but feel very uncomfortable. There's something here with us, in this shadowy house, and it's not human. I can feel it slinking about just out of sight.

"He claimed that Kafka, for example, was on the side of evil because of what and how he wrote," says Isabella, she of the giant earrings, heavy makeup and 1970s polyester pantsuits. "And so he felt guilty about it. I'm sure Kafka felt some guilt but it wasn't because he believed he was on the side of evil. It's a ludicrous stance, so as much as I adore you, my dear, I have to agree with Jeffrey on this one."

Dario playfully rolls his eyes, then takes a sip of wine. "You've got to go home with him, so of course you do!"

"Well, I don't *have* to!"

As the three burst into laughter and Remy and I play along, Sue emerges from the kitchen carrying a small tray of cheese and crackers and places it on the coffee table. "What sort of mischief are you up to now?" she asks her husband in her typically squeaky voice.

"You know me," Dario says, slipping an arm around his wife's tiny waist and drawing her closer, "always up to no good."

Isabella selects a cracker and nibbles. "Why so quiet tonight, Remy?"

"Just taking it all in," she says with her usual flair.

"Planning a sneak attack, no doubt," Dario says with a grin.

As they continue talking, my discomfort increases, so I drift away, moving subtly toward the other side of the room, where another couple, Leigh and Wayne, sit on a love seat in front of a vast bookcase. While Leigh works at the school with Remy and the others, her husband Wayne is an executive at a clothing store chain, and like me, attends these things purely as labors of love. I find both he and Leigh easier to talk with and much more down to earth, so I continue my slow escape until I've reached them.

Wayne looks up from what was a quiet conversation with his wife and flashes a brilliant smile. "Bailing on the Baudelaire debate, huh? Whoever the hell that is."

"I somehow managed to tear myself away."

Leigh, a statuesque woman with Nordic features and blonde hair so light it's nearly white, smiles at me with what appears to be considerable effort. "You timed it perfectly," she tells me. "They'll be talking shop in no time, and that's even worse, trust me."

I smile politely. "Hope you don't mind me interrupting you guys."

"Not interrupting at all," Wayne answers. Always impeccably dressed in suits and ties, he has the square-jawed and somewhat vacuous good looks of a movie star, and although he and

Leigh are about five or six years younger than the rest of us, I've always found them far more intelligent, interesting and witty than the others. "We were beginning to feel a little left out."

"If I wanted to discuss Baudelaire, I could," Leigh informs us. "But it's been a long week. I'm not up for one of Dario's debates tonight."

"Let's talk football and really freak him out," Wayne suggests.

Leigh, laughing lightly, gives her husband a playful slap on the arm.

"Organized sport is about nothing more than the male organ," Wayne says, quietly doing his best Dario impersonation, "and the exploitation of minority youth."

"Stop," Leigh says in a loud whisper, "you're terrible. Dario means well."

"He does?" The words spill from my mouth before I can stop them.

"Nice." Wayne raises his glass to me in mock salute.

"He's not so bad," Leigh says. "It's just his way."

"And what's up with these tunes?" Wayne mumbles, referring to the classical music playing softly from speakers hidden somewhere in the room. "Sounds like a funeral dirge, for Christ's sake."

"*Wayne*," Leigh says, this time gripping his arm. "Stop, honey, seriously."

Since Leigh and Wayne are the only ones among us who have children, to deflect the conversation away from our host I ask how their two sons are doing. Leigh responds by unleashing a tsunami of information, gleefully updating me on their activities and accomplishments. Thankfully Wayne rescues me by asking how my job's going. I give him the standard answer and the small talk continues. I struggle to stay focused, but my mind is elsewhere, and my eyes are drawn to the windows again and again, as if there's something out there that needs my attention as well.

In time more people arrive, filling the house with several

couples I've never met. With my head fogging over and my body beginning to feel sluggish, my eyes drift through the growing horde until I locate Remy on the other side of the room chatting with Isabella and another woman I don't know. She sees me and gives a rather guilty smile, as if to say she hadn't realized so many people would be coming. I offer a subtle shrug, then turn back to Wayne and Leigh, who don't seem to notice I haven't been listening to them for the last few seconds.

Leigh suddenly excuses herself and slips away through the crowd, disappearing upstairs, presumably to use the bathroom.

"Let's get another drink." Wayne rises from the love seat. "Come on, we can't be expected to face these people sober."

I look into my glass. Melting ice. "Think I'm going to pass, thanks."

"Suit yourself," he says, moving away.

A young woman with deathly pale skin, dreadlocks, several tattoos and sad, dark eyes outfitted with black liner and shadow separates from a small group of people to my left. She looks wildly out of place here, more like a student than another teacher or contemporary of our hosts. Silver earrings in the shape of crosses dangle from her ears, catching the low light from a nearby lamp. She walks by and smiles at me in a way that seems almost familiar. I nod and smile back. Dressed in a loose but heavy gray sweater, jeans and knee-high black boots, she stops as if planning to speak to me, but then seems to think better of it and walks on, taking up position in front of one of the windows facing the street.

Outside, a very light snow has begun to fall.

I head for the couch and locate my wife not far from where I last saw her. She, Isabella and the other woman are chatting, but Remy excuses herself from their conversation just as I arrive and joins me instead, slipping her arm around my waist.

"You okay?" she asks softly.

"Fine, you guys get the whole Baudelaire thing worked out?"

Remy rolls her eyes and sips her wine.

"I thought it was just going to be a few people?"

135

"That's what I was told," she says. "Want to get going?"

"Would you mind? I'm still not feeling well."

Remy smiles and gives me a peck on the cheek. "Sue's been putting coats upstairs on their bed, I'll go grab ours."

"I'll get them. You let Sue know we're leaving, okay?"

As I start for the stairs, Remy gently touches my arm. "Are you all right, Cam?"

"No, I told you I'm not feeling well."

"But is there something…more?"

"I'd just like to go home, lie down and get some rest, okay?"

"Oh, look," Remy says, pointing toward the windows with a bright, childlike smile. "It's snowing. How beautiful, isn't it—sweetie—isn't it beautiful?"

I glance over my shoulder, see the snow falling through darkness. The woman with the dreadlocks is gone. "Yeah, it's… yes, it is." I casually search the room but cannot locate her. How could she have vanished so quickly?

Remy touches my forehead. "You're a little warm again."

"I'll go get the coats."

As I move through the room, excusing myself as I go, everything seems to change. Nothing seems right. The people, their faces, the sounds of their voices; none of it seems as it should be, but rather distorted, corrupted somehow. There is darkness here, and it is slowly draping itself over the entire house and everyone in it, absorbing and changing everything. My heart races and my palms begin to sweat. Why is it suddenly so goddamn warm in here?

I slip into a short hallway, turn to my right and ascend the stairs. A winding staircase leads me to another short hallway with a series of doors on either side of it and a single door at the very end I know to be the bathroom. There is a light fixture overhead but I can't seem to locate a switch. The only light comes from an open door about halfway down the hallway, a small swath of dull yellow spilling free. The other doors are closed, so I assume the open one must be Sue and Dario's bedroom.

Downstairs a burst of cackling laughter erupts, followed by the hum of numerous voices. I look back, but I've gone too far down the hallway and can no longer see the bottom of the staircase.

"Come on!" a woman's voice yells from downstairs, and suddenly the soft classical music is replaced with something far more sinister in tone, a raging guitar riff that is so loud it shakes the entire house. A booming bassline follows, then a pounding drumbeat and vocals that sound more like the growls of an animal than the singing of a human being. More laughter wafts up the stairs as the volume of people's voices increases to compensate for the deafening music.

Temples pounding, I close my eyes and rub them a moment.

There is danger here. I'm in danger, Remy's in danger. We have to get out.

I open my eyes and move quickly for the open door. As I approach, I can see someone standing on the far side of the bed, which is covered in an enormous pile of coats and jackets. I hesitate just outside the doorway. The person has her back to me but the dreadlocks give her away. How did she get up here before me, and without ever passing by me in the living room?

The sound of another door opening turns my attention to the end of the hallway. The bathroom door slowly swings open to reveal Leigh standing just inside. She is completely nude and has a baffled look on her face. At her feet, on the tile floor, is a fresh pile of excrement. She looks at me and cocks her head as if confused. Urine seeps from between her legs, running down onto the floor in a steady stream.

I take a step back, unable to believe what I'm seeing.

"Leigh?" My voice sounds foreign to me as it drifts down the dim hallway.

Her upper lip trembles into a snarl but she makes no sound. Blue eyes suddenly dark, she steps forward, grabs the door and slams it shut.

The music downstairs continues, pounding in time with the throbbing in my temples. I look to the bedroom. The young woman is still there, only she's looking right at me now with her black eyes, the dreads hanging on either side of her face like dead snakes and her earrings swaying as she slowly rocks her head back and forth.

"Where am I?" I ask her.

"Closer," she says in a smoky voice.

My eyes fill with tears of horror and fear. Ashamed, I angrily wipe them away. "Closer to what?"

"Home."

"Who are you?"

"A warrior," she tells me, "the same as you."

"I'm no warrior."

"You think the war stops for you? It never stops."

Fear becomes rage. "I don't know what the fuck you're talking about!"

Suddenly something smashes into the window behind her with a hideous thud, startling me. The woman never looks back, but a large black bird has crashed into the window and now lies twitching on the sill, a smear of blood splashed against the pane. After a moment, another bird crashes into the window and falls away into the night, blood spraying and falling through the darkness amidst an ocean of snowflakes.

A smile slowly creeps across her face. "They're dying for you, Zeke."

Behind me, something unseen scurries down the hallway. Something small.

My hands ball into fists, and through gritted teeth I tell her my name is Cameron Horne. "I'm not who you think I am."

"Maybe you're not who you think you are."

Another noise behind me draws my attention back to the staircase. A middle-aged man I've never seen before is huddled a few steps from the top of the stairs, peeking at me through the balusters, his dark eyes wild as if possessed and his face twisted into a hideously demonic grin. He begins to laugh. It is a horrible sound.

But he's not looking at me. He's looking past me.

I follow his gaze. Crawling along the hallway...on the floor, the walls and, impossibly, the ceilings...children...horribly mutilated, deformed and bloody nude children, lost little lambs damned to a Hell they should be nowhere near, that they should have no concept of or—no—no—not children but...something *like* children, grunting and snorting, pigs at a trough. Their eyes—my God—their eyes, what—what's happened to their eyes, all white and glistening, no iris, no pupil, what—what have they done to their eyes?

I step into the bedroom, close the door behind me and lean back against it, watching the woman with dreadlocks throughout. "What's happening to me?"

"You're dying."

"Dying? I—what—what do you mean?"

She raises her hands and opens them, showing me her palms. Tattooed across one is the sigil of Baphomet, and the other bears a satanic cross. "You're dying," she says again. "Slowly... gradually...and as before, as *always*, with death comes life. Who should know that better than you?"

"I don't want to die."

The woman lowers her hands. "I know."

"Who are you?"

She watches me but doesn't answer.

"I've seen you before, haven't I?" I ask. "Another place, maybe...another time...why can't I remember?"

"Do you *want* to remember?"

"Yes. How do I know you? Where have I seen you before?"

"Where the rainbow ends," she says.

"I don't understand. What does that mean?" Something scratches at the door, sending a chill of terror through me. I lean more of my weight against it. "What have I done? What have I done to make this happen?"

The woman moves around the side of the bed, her gait slinky and sexy now as she makes her way closer to me. Stopping just inches away, she leans in, brushes her lips against my ear and whispers, "You exist."

Dropping to her knees before me, she reaches for my belt and undoes my pants.

"It's all right," she tells me, squeezing me and pulling me free. "It's all right now."

"Please don't," I tell her, but my voice is weak, the words are slurred and I can already feel her warm, wet mouth suckling me as I grow hard between her lips.

Fuck her throat until she pukes. Fuck that little slut's mouth until—

"No!"

I push her away, yank open the door and stagger into the hallway, expecting to see the man from the stairs and the hideous little beings waiting for me. But they're not there. The music increases in volume as I stumble toward the staircase, and as I reach the top of the stairs I stop and look down through the darkness to the short hallway below. I can see one corner of the living room. Some partygoers are standing and talking, others dance furiously to the thrashing guitars and hammering drums. Remy is nowhere in sight.

Looking back down the hallway, I see that the bathroom door is still closed, but there is something moving in there, I can see something moving beneath the door, something wet and slithering and alive, a hideous tentaclelike appendage poking out and snaking along the carpet as if for purchase.

Fumbling with my zipper and belt until they're back in place, I force myself down the stairs, taking them at a tremendous pace and nearly falling several times before I reach the bottom. Frantic, I want nothing more than to find Remy and get as far away from this house as possible, but I am immediately assaulted by the raucous music and the loud voices of the partygoers. The house is crowded with people, a sea of them surging and dancing as if under the control of something demonic, their faces and bodies twisted and jerking about, writhing like pieces of a greater whole.

Calling Remy's name, I push my way through the crowd, but I don't see her anywhere. In fact, I cannot locate anyone I know or even recognize, yet nearly all of the people in the room stop and tug at me or smile and say things to me as if they know exactly who I am, their voices indecipherable amidst the raging music. I keep on, disoriented and struggling through waves of dancers, but still, Remy is nowhere to be found.

"Remy!"

My head reels. Fearful I might pass out, I whirl around on shaky legs, my shoulders knocking aside the partygoers that surround me, their faces and bodies flying by in a blur, their laughter and voices a steady hums beneath the powerful driving music.

And then the entire room is spinning out of control, everything distorted and indistinct, dizzying, a carnival ride gone wild.

"Remy!"

We're coming for you...

"Remy, where are you!"

I close my eyes, and it feels like I've taken flight, or perhaps left my body entirely.

You can't stop it...

My eyes open, the room tilts and I realize I'm falling.

You can't save her...

I land hard, on my back, the air knocked from my lungs in one violent rush.

You can't even save yourself...

And the dancers are coming closer, closing the circle, their feet stomping and moving all around me, stepping on me, kicking at me. I struggle to get up onto all fours, but they surge closer, knocking me back onto my side. The music is so loud, so strong I—I want it to stop. It's tearing my skull apart.

"Remy! Remy, help me!"

Amidst the forest of gyrating legs and feet, a closer look reveals that some do not belong to human beings, but things that more closely resemble hoofs. Goats, there are goats here, their horns long and dark and curled, beady dead eyes staring at me blankly through the throng of dancers.

A nude man a few feet away crawls along the floor, his body and face slick with blood. He looks at me and laughs, his white teeth startling against the crimson backdrop. He says something but I can't hear him above the din of music and growling vocals.

Someone steps on him, the heel of their shoe stomping the small of his back. Blood erupts from the man's mouth but he laughs, wide-eyed with excitement.

I am kicked in the ribs—hard—and I try again to get to my feet despite the sharp pain that rockets from my midsection up into my armpit.

And then someone grabs hold of me and pulls me to my feet. "Cam, can you hear me?"

God help me.

Remy, is it—is it Remy?

There is no God here.

And then it is quiet and I am spinning...turning...falling...tumbling through unimaginable darkness...spiraling away slowly...a dead body drifting through the soundless vacuum of space.

There is nothing here.

Never have I been so completely alone.

A voice, faint but audible, slowly emerges from the darkness. I know that voice.

It's my own.

"Hello?"

It's me, I...I'm alive. I'm alive!

"Hello?"

Wind...is that wind?

"Hello!"

No. Breathing, it's—it's breathing, someone breathing in my ear.

A flash of light, a piercing high-pitched pain stabbing my temple, and then I'm standing before an end table in my great room, the cordless phone in my hand.

The line goes dead. A dial tone sounds and I drop the phone.

It crashes against the floor as I stagger toward the bar.

I don't make it.

Later, Remy finds me cowering in our bedroom closet.

"You're having nightmares, sweetheart," she assures me, leading me back to bed and holding me in her arms, "terrible, terrible nightmares."

I suspect most women confronted with such dramatics would react differently, but not Remy, not my beautiful, loving Remy.

"And that's all they are, Cam. That's all they are."

I want so very much to believe her.

She lies down with me and gently strokes my forehead until I finally allow sleep to take me, my face nestled snugly against her breasts.

I dream of nothing. I dream of Hell.

CHAPTER TEN

Come morning, I awaken to the sound of the car alarm. Remy is gone, but the young man is waiting for me out by the fire pit in the backyard, just as I knew he would be. I step outside and cross the yard. I swear it snowed the night before, but there is no trace of it, no signs. Instead, I find a chilly and overcast morning.

The young man sees me, pulls his cigarettes from his jacket pocket and holds the pack and a lighter out for me. He looks worse than the last time I saw him, paler, thinner, sickly. "Figured since you started again you might want one," he tells me.

I'm too exhausted and battered to argue with him, so I take the cigarettes, light one, then hand them back. "How do you know the things you know?"

He shrugs.

"You know the future, and things you couldn't possibly know. How do you do it?"

"Perspective," Mac says. "If you stand over an anthill watching the ants go about their daily lives, you know what you know not because you have special powers, but because of your perspective. You've got a God's-eye view—best seat in the house—and one that allows you to see things those ants can't, things you see and understand long before they do. Doesn't mean you're a god; just observant."

"But you're not just an observer. You're a part of this too, aren't you?"

"In a way."

"You know what that's all about?" I ask, motioning to the woods and the whining car alarm.

He takes a drag on his cigarette and exhales through his nose. As the smoke dissipates, a slow trickle of blood begins to leak from his left nostril. "Yeah," he replies, "I do."

"You're bleeding," I tell him.

He flicks the cigarette away and wipes the blood from his face with his fingers. A second trickle replaces the first but he seems not to care. "She's not going to call," he says. "You need to go to her."

"Who?"

"Marianne." His right nostril begins to bleed. "She wants to call, but she won't."

"Mac, you're *bleeding*."

"She's so afraid she doesn't know what to do," he says. "She knows the truth."

"About what's happening to me?"

"Go to her. You don't have much time."

"Is she all right?"

"No one's all right."

I watch him bleed. "Tell me who you are."

"My name's McEnroe," he says. "You know, like the tennis player. Only it's spelled a little different."

The car alarm stops.

"Am I in Hell?" I ask.

Mac shakes his head. "Not yet."

* * *

On an unassuming side street in a quiet residential neighbor-hood in South Boston, I find Marianne's first-floor apartment. Located in a double-decker, I once picked her up out in front when she was training and we were doing field work, but I've not been back since and have never been inside. Now, with a gentle rain falling, I sit in my car and watch her building for sev-eral minutes, taking note of the street and surrounding houses and apartments as well. An elderly man moves along the street with an umbrella in one hand and a bag of groceries in the other, but otherwise, the street is empty. Marianne's car is parked a few spaces away.

Moving quickly, I take the steps and slip in through the front door. I find myself in a small foyer, a staircase directly in front of me and doors to separate apartments on either side of it. I know hers is the one to the left, so I locate a doorbell alongside the casing and press that. When no one answers, I knock.

The door swings open.

Craning my neck, I step through the opening but can't see much. "Marianne? It's me, Cam."

No answer.

"Marianne?" I call again. "Are you there? It's Cam."

I move farther inside.

The apartment is small, cluttered, decorated in a dated man-ner one might expect from a much older woman, and smells like potpourri. I step directly into a living room, close the door behind me and venture deeper into the apartment.

I do not have to go far before I find Marianne sitting on the floor alongside a large couch. Dressed in a pair of sweatpants, a T-shirt and white socks, she stares right at me but there is no recognition, no life or light in her at all, and at first I think she's dead.

"Marianne?" I say, softly now.

Her emerald eyes blink once…twice, and she slowly cocks her head, obviously seeing me for the first time. Brows furrowed, she grimaces and shakes her head no. "You can't...You can't be here," she says, her voice raspy and raw, weak.

"Are you all right?" I ask, crouching down but keeping some distance.

She looks at me as if I'm crazy.

I notice a bottle of Jack Daniel's lying empty and on its side on the floor next to her. Alongside it is a prescription drug bottle for some sort of anti-anxiety pill. In her lap is a 9mm handgun.

"Marianne, why do you have a gun?"

"I'm from a family of cops," she says, her eyes filling with tears. "I grew up around them. I know how to handle them."

"Why is it in your lap?"

She smiles but it's not her typical grin. This is something different, something bleak and hopeless. Slowly, she raises the gun to her temple.

"Don't," I say, holding my hands up like this might help. "Marianne, look at me. Don't. Put the gun down, okay? Just put it down and we'll talk."

She chuckles joylessly and drops her hand back to her lap. "You really still believe it matters?"

"Of course it matters. What happened?"

"You were right. Had one of my brothers do a full run on Copeland, and there's absolutely nothing on him beyond the dates we had. It's like he came into existence suddenly and without any prior history." She leans toward me, eyes wide and still glistening. "And do you know why that is? Because before then he didn't fucking exist. Only that's impossible, right? You know, except for the part where apparently it isn't."

Never before have I seen her so physically and psychologically devastated. "How long have you been up?"

"All night. Relatively sure I won't ever sleep again."

"Did you drink that entire bottle of Jack?"

She glances at it with contempt. "Evidently."

"How many of those pills did you take?"

"Let's say more than two."

"Give me the gun, Marianne."

"Yeah, definitely not gonna do that." She takes it from her lap and holds it down against the side of her leg to illustrate the point. "Just get out. Run while you still can. It's your only chance."

"I can't leave you alone like this."

"You don't have a choice."

"Let me help you."

"You can't."

Something slithers quickly along the floor and into a dark hallway on the far side of the room before I can clearly see what it is. I regain my feet, distracted by more movement through the shadows along the walls, in the corners.

"I have to get you out of here," I tell her. "It's not safe here."

"It's not safe anywhere. I figured this had to be some sort of elaborate mistake, right? So I went to see your boy Copeland and find out for myself."

My heart plummets. "No."

"Oh yes." A dark cloud passes across her pale face. "And he showed me things, Cam…things no one should ever fucking see."

I can feel my anger rising. "Did he hurt you? What did he do?"

"It's all a lie," she says flatly. "And you know it."

"I told you to stay away from him."

"Yes, you did." Marianne's eyes move and slide about as if she's lost control of them. They seem to return to her, but when they do, they're dead. "He knows the truth. He knows all of it."

"Copeland's a bag of shit. A sexual predator that—"

"He knows the goddamn truth!" she snaps. "And he knows you."

"What did he tell you?"

"Did you hear me? He *knows* you."

I know you, Horne.

"He knows nothing."

"He knows everything." Marianne turns away, no longer on

the verge of tears but complete collapse. "Go home, Cam. Go home."

"I just came from there, I—"

"No," she says, "your childhood home. Go home and talk to your parents."

A once vibrant and strong woman looks up at me, transformed into someone on the verge of slipping into a coma, someone destroyed, shattered, and beyond repair. I know then that she's right. I can't save her. I never could. And I'm sorry, so very sorry.

Because I know I will never see her again.

"My parents are dead."

Outside, the rain picks up, spraying the windows. Marianne's apartment suddenly feels more like a tomb, a place of death and emptiness, of misery.

She smiles sadly as the shadows behind her move, creeping about like the dark lords they are. "What difference does that make?"

* * *

From the darkness, Anthony…his beady black rat eyes glaring at me from his now skeletal, pale, pockmarked face…

Still dressed in his tuxedo, it was now soiled and wet and covered in filth the same as I was. And just like me, he stunk. I could smell his foul stench even though he was several feet away. Smiling that condescendingly evil smile, he strode toward me.

"We've made it, sir," he said. "We've made it."

And then I remembered him dragging me through the sewers beneath the nightclub to these strange and forgotten old ruins of what appeared to have once been a luxurious hotel. "I want to leave this place, Anthony."

He pointed at something behind me. "Then go ahead, sir."

Although terrified, I forced myself to look back over my shoulder. The rickety old elevator from my nightmares and visions awaited me.

"No..."

"They're waiting for you, Mr. Horne."

I knew the moment I stepped inside and the doors closed, the cable would snap like always and the elevator would plummet, rocketing down the shaft and vanishing into the bottomless pit below. "I won't go."

"But they're waiting for you," Anthony repeated. *"They've been waiting so very long, sir."*

Somewhere outside that strange dark building, the rain continued to fall as thunder rumbled in the heavens.

A bell sounded and the elevator doors rattled open.

Inside, the faceless operator stood at the ready.

With a formal and dramatic bow, Anthony backed away and into the darkness from which he'd come.

Then up from the shaft and out through that old elevator came thousands of snarling voices nowhere near human, a battle cry of ancient brutal warriors there to fetch me for their depraved master. Dead or alive.

* * *

Dorchester, in the rain, on a dilapidated porch littered with bags of rotting trash. The same plastic bowl as before lies inches from my feet, but the orange cat is nowhere to be found. The dark and dirty duplex sits silent in the downpour, lifeless and hiding its secrets, but not for long.

This time the locks disengage even before I knock, the door creaks open and Alfred Copeland stands before me, his plump form draped in a loose T-shirt several sizes too large for him. His legs and feet are bare, his toes crooked and caked with dirt, his toenails long and discolored. He is unshaven, and the hair jutting out on either side of his otherwise bald head is unwashed and unruly as ever. The eyes too are the same as before. Empty...broken...lost...drowning in things unclean...evil.

Without a word, he steps to the side and lazily motions for me to enter.

Once I'm inside, he closes the door, then leads me to the kitchen. It is the same mess it was the first time I came here, but this time the doors to the adjacent bedroom and bathroom are both closed. But for a rickety kitchen table and chairs, there is still no furniture here, and dingy sheets remain tacked up over the windows instead of curtains.

Copeland takes up position on the other side of the table and stands there as if already bored with my presence. His depravity hangs in the air between us like fog.

"Why don't you do us both a favor and go put some pants on?" I tell him.

"Why don't you go fuck yourself?"

"Trust me, Copeland, you don't want to make me any angrier than I already am."

"You think I'm afraid of you?" He smiles with his yellow, decayed, crooked teeth. "Is that what you think?"

"You should be."

"You're the one who should be afraid."

"What did you do to Marianne?"

His eyes dart to the closed bedroom door, then back to me. "I told her the truth."

"Are we alone here?"

He slowly shakes his head no.

My heart begins to race. "Is there someone in the bedroom?"

"You know," he says, "many have done this before me. Many have done it before you. Only it's usually to their advantage, to further evil, and even then we don't get away with it. We always end up right back where we started. Difference is we don't much care, because that's where we belong. Just some wolves out playing in the night and home to the den before sunrise, that's all. But not you though. Oh no, not you. You're something special. Who the hell do you think you are, Horne?"

"Is there someone in that bedroom, you son of a bitch?"

His soulless eyes watch me. "They're just playthings, toys. But you seem to think they matter. Delusions of fucking grandeur, that's your problem."

Thunder booms as rain pounds the house, coming down in sheets now and blurring the already filthy windows. Like before, things begin to shift, to feel more like a dream. Slower... imprecise...distorted...

"I know you," Copeland tells me. "I *know* you, Horne. And you know me."

"Until I came here to do my job, we'd never met before."

"No?"

"No."

He laughs lightly and scratches at his crotch. "There are always boundaries, you know that. In all of nature, there are always boundaries. And when they're crossed, things have to be set right, or the entire thing can come crashing down. Couldn't have that, could we? None of the powers that be are gonna sit still for that bullshit. Because it's all about order, even the chaos, right? You're no savior. You're not even a dime novel hero, Horne. You're just a rogue male, that's all, a freak. You're an aberration even among deviants. And you know what happens to rogue males, no matter what the species? Sooner or later they get put down. Either an outside species or their own takes care of them, because they're out of order. Saw a show one time in the joint, one of those nature shows about lions. You know the kind I mean. Followed this pride around, mostly focusing on this one mother and her cubs. Outside the pride, there was this rogue male hanging around causing trouble, breaking the rules. It stalked the cubs for days but always stayed on the perimeter of the pride's territory. Until one day, it attacked. It charged the cubs. The mother defended her babies, her way of life. She defended the *rules*. She threw herself between her offspring and that rogue male and she fought back with everything she had. Even though she drove him off before he could kill any of the cubs, the pride realized this lion was too much of a wild card, too much of a threat. It might've been one of their own at some point but it wasn't like them anymore. It was rogue. So it had to go. Next time it ventured too close, they took it the fuck *out*." Copeland slaps his hands down on the table with a resounding thud. "You better get on your knees, boy, and pray to your lord before that happens to you."

I stare at him, unmoved by his theatrics. "What about you, Copeland?"

He straightens up. "What about me?"

"Aren't you the real rogue male here? You're the one snatching little girls off—"

"You fucking fool," he says. "When a lion takes down and eats a beautiful gazelle, it's just a lion being a lion. I still know who I am. I still know my place."

"You're nothing but a pedophile, a sexual sadist, a rapist of little girls."

"Every now and then I make an exception, give an older one a good fuck," he says, waiting for my reaction before adding, "you know, like Remy."

Visions of the nightclub stage blink through my mind.

"That wasn't real, how did you—how do you—that wasn't real!"

I'm going to kill him. You know that, don't you?

"You're a fucking imbecile."

You're so silly tonight, Mr. Horne. You already have.

I move around the side of the table, closer to him. "You don't even speak her name, you understand me? You don't even *think* about her, you piece of fucking shit!"

"Yeah, I'm a piece of shit. And what are you, Horne, any idea?"

"I'm the one who's going to put *you* down, that's what I am."

He nods, drifts away from the table and moves over to a counter. Leaning back against a sink full of dirty dishes, he folds his arms across his chest. "Toll's due," he says evenly. "But you won't be the one to make me pay it."

We stand in silence for what seems a very long time.

"You need to go home, Horne," he finally says. "You hear me? Go home."

Go home and talk to your parents.

Instead, I start slowly toward the bedroom.

My parents are dead.

"Sure you want to go in there?" Copeland asks but makes no move to stop me.

What difference does that make?

"Think you can handle it, Mary?" he goads.

The doorknob is cold in my hand. "What have you done?" I ask quietly.

"Just being a lion, baby, just being a lion."

I turn the knob, then give the door a subtle push. With a creaking sound, it slowly swings open. A strong rancid odor wafts free. Tacked up over the only window is another towel, and the rest of the small room is draped in shadow and half-light. As before, there is only a bare and filthy mattress lying on the floor, some pornographic magazines and spent rolls of toilet paper scattered about.

But this time there is a pile of clothes on the mattress, clothes that clearly belong to a young girl. Copeland releases an orgasmic sigh before he begins whispering his profane, inverted prayers.

"Heaven in art who Father our..."

In my mind I see the girl's tiny arms tied behind her with rope, her ankles bound as well, her nude body covered in lacerations, bruises and welts, her hair caked with blood.

"Name thy be hallowed..."

There's no need to look any closer. The clothes are soiled with blood and other bodily fluids, some hers, some his.

"Done be will thy, come kingdom thy..."

Whoever the little girl was, I'm certain she's dead, as the mattress too is soaked with blood.

"Heaven in is it as Earth on..."

"You want to vomit," Copeland says from somewhere behind me. "But you won't. You want to cry, but you can't. We're the same, you and me."

"Where is she?" I ask, still staring at the clothes.

"They'll find her eventually...what's left of her anyway." He snickers. "I knew I didn't have much time, figured I'd better kick it up a notch."

My hands shake with rage and sorrow.

"You ever see the vampire movies where a bunch of blood-suckers close in on someone who just got bit? And just before they kill him, they slowly back off, because they understand now that he's turned, he's one of them. You may want to put me down, Horne, but you won't, because you're one of us."

I step back out of the bedroom and close the door behind me. "Even if that was true," I say, feeling the evil moving deep within me, "I'm a rogue male, remember?"

Unsure of me, his gleeful blasphemy fades.

"I don't follow the rules." I remove my jacket, hang it over the back of one of the kitchen chairs, then methodically roll my shirtsleeves up to the elbow. On the counter is a half-eaten sandwich, a can of ginger ale, a jar of mayonnaise and a silver butter knife. I select the knife, hold it up before me and study the dull blade. When my eyes find Copeland, he understands I've decided this will do just fine.

Rain batters the building, sealing us in tight and drowning out the screams of agony and horror that will soon shatter the silence of Alfred Copeland's apartment.

"I'm out of order," I tell him. "Remember?"

Copeland steels himself, contemptible until the end. "I remember nothing."

"You're gonna remember this, motherfucker."

Now, the gleeful blasphemy belongs to me.

CHAPTER ELEVEN

The wind is strong, forcefully rolling along the avenues as I drive through my hometown, the city of Fall River. Although the rain has all but subsided by the time I arrive there, just a little over an hour since leaving Dorchester, the same dingy industrial pale hangs over this section of city as always, echoes of a once thriving textiles trade that is long gone but still lingers like a ghost in the shadow of the nearby Braga Bridge.

After what I've done, I don't know if I'll ever be able to go home again. Can I ever again look Remy in the face, hold her in my arms and tell her I love her? How do I go back? How do I forget this and make it go away? Is that even possible? Whoever this is walking around in my skin and claiming to be me is not Cameron Horne. It's some other man, one who enjoys and is skilled at inflicting pain, someone intimately familiar and comfortable with violence, bloodshed, carnage and agony. Death. This thing inside me is its messenger, and I am its vessel.

I bind him with belts I find in the bedroom. He is so badly beaten by then that he offers little resistance. A naked blob jiggling and bleeding all over a scarred floor, his blood mixing with his victim's, Copeland refuses to make a sound. He thinks he will rob me of the satisfaction of hearing him scream and beg for mercy. He's wrong.

I find my old neighborhood quickly. A few of the buildings and businesses have changed here and there, but for the most part, it's the same as it was when I was a kid, and a flood of memories surge through me as I turn onto my old street and slowly roll toward the triple-decker that housed the apartment I grew up in with my parents. My blood is still running cold, but memories of playing on this street, of learning how to ride a bike on these very sidewalks, of growing up here and all the history and experiences I enjoyed in this neighborhood keep coming.

I find a small radio on the windowsill and switch it on. An old '50s tune crackles through the cheap speaker. Del Shannon singing "My Little Runaway": "My little runaway, run-run-run-runaway! I'm walkin' in the rain. Tears are fallin' and I feel the pain!"—and I hesitate a moment, allowing the music to move me. Soon, I'm dancing along, smiling down at Copeland as I fondle the butter knife I plan to mutilate him with. His swollen and bloodied eyes widen in horror, but he still refuses to make a sound, even when I kneel down next to him and, with the rhythm of the music, slam the dull blade up under his arm, piercing the flesh there before plunging deep enough to hit bone.

After finding a space, I exit the car and walk briskly to the building, hands stuffed in my jacket pockets. There are a few people milling about the neighborhood, along with some light traffic, but I pay little attention as I tentatively climb the steps of the building. It has undergone some modest remodeling and updates over the years, but our first-floor apartment basically looks the same. I've no idea who lives here now, but I draw a deep breath and knock anyway.

Warm and sticky, Copeland's blood sprays my hands, arms and neck. And now he cries and begs like there's no tomorrow—because there isn't one—his life is slipping away slowly, painfully, and there isn't a fucking thing he can do to stop it. He tries to tell me something, but I've already taken off most of his bottom lip so it's impossible to know for sure what he's saying. Using the small, mildly serrated section of blade, I saw away strips of flesh from his stomach, chest, arms and legs, then roll him over and get to work on his back. I wonder if the little girl he murdered cried and squirmed the way he does.

I hear movement from within, a shuffling of feet, then the sounds of locks disengaging. My heart races with anticipation. The door opens, answered by an elderly man in a cardigan sweater and a pair of slacks. His features are soft and rounded, his thin gray hair parted on the side and neatly combed into place. He raises his bushy white eyebrows at the sight of me. "Yes?"

As I wash up in the bathroom, I glance in the dirty mirror over the sink, see Copeland's body behind me on the kitchen floor. He's dead, has been for several minutes. But I am grateful that he was alive long enough to feel me hack and rip his cock from his body and force it deep into his mangled mouth.

"I'm sorry to bother you," I tell the old man. "My name's Cameron Horne, I used to live in this apartment. I grew up here."

"Who is it?" a female voice asks from behind the man.

Rather than answer her, the man says, "I'm sorry, you—you're *who?*"

"Cameron Horne. I used to live here years ago."

"Sam, who is it?" the woman asks again.

"A young man," he says, glancing back over his shoulder a moment before returning his attention to me. "You say you lived here?"

I realize I have no idea what the hell I'm doing here, why I'm bothering these people or why they'd care what I have to say.

"Yes, sir," I answer, suddenly worried I might not have washed all of Copeland's blood from my hands, "when I was a child."

The man squints at me. "What did you say your name was again?"

"Cameron Horne."

"Which apartment did you live in?"

"This one," I tell him.

"When you were a child, you say?"

"Yes, sir, I grew up on this street."

He smiles at me warmly. "I'm afraid you've got the wrong building."

"No, this—this is the place."

"Can't be," he says. "My wife and I have lived here for the last forty-seven years. You can't even be that old, are you?"

I step back, more a nervous reaction than anything else, and quickly locate the number to the right of the door just to make sure. "That's not possible."

"Exactly, son, that's what I'm trying to tell you."

"What's going on? What is this?"

"You've got the wrong building, kiddo, it happens, nothing to get upset about."

"But I don't have the wrong building. This is it."

The woman, presumably Sam's wife, appears behind him, craning her neck for a look at the man at their door. A short but robust woman, she wears an inordinate amount of makeup and an inexpensive wig far too large for her head.

"Sadie, let me handle this," Sam says.

Smiling at me with obvious dentures, she says, "We've lived here for years."

The fear is rising, growing stronger, bordering on panic. "Look, I know the building and the apartment I grew up in, all right? This is it."

"Son," Sam says, "what is it we can do for you?"

Equal doses of panic, confusion and desperation take hold of me. I'm lost in a dream. That must be it, I'm dreaming. "I don't even know why I'm here, but I...I know this building, I know this apartment, this street and this neighborhood."

They look at me with what I'm sure is pity.

"I learned to ride a bike right there," I say, pointing to the street. "I—I used to buy Cokes and candy bars and comic books at the store on the corner there. It looked different then…there was a—a grill and lunch counter in the back. Mr. Hodges owned it, a nice old man who used to make the best chocolate milk-shakes and cheeseburgers in town. Mrs. Larson lived upstairs in this building and she…I…my friends lived in that building right over there, and we used to play and have sleepovers and… my mother and I used to sit in this apartment and she'd read and I'd…I can show you the room, I—I can show you exactly where it was. I used to sit on these steps—these very steps— and wait for my father to come home." Everything is crushing me, hitting me all at once, and none of it makes a goddamn bit of sense. "This was my life, do you understand? This was my childhood home. I grew up here, I…"

Sadie smiles at me with what appears to be genuine sympathy. "Young man, you're mistaken. You never lived here."

I slam my hand against the door casing. "This is bullshit!"

"Hey now," the old man says. "Careful there, what are you trying to do?"

"And such language," Sadie sighs, shakes her head and fingers a silver broach in the shape of a goat pinned to her blouse.

The man aims an arthritically crooked finger at me. "You watch your mouth. There's a lady present."

I flex my hands, my body twitching and jerking about like some sort of mental patient. "Why are you lying to me?"

Sadie leans close to her husband and whispers, "Poor baby doesn't know yet."

"What?" I ask. "What did you just say?"

"Quiet, Sadie."

"But he doesn't know, he obviously doesn't know yet, he—"

"I said be quiet!" Sam snaps.

The woman shuffles back into the apartment and out of view.

After a moment, Sam takes a step out and joins me on the stoop. There is something wrong about this old man. "I think it'd be best if you just go on about your business. You never lived here."

"What don't I know yet? What don't I know?"

The man steps back into the apartment. "You take care, Zeke."

Shivers fire across my shoulders and up into my neck. "I told you my name was Cameron Horne, why did you call me Zeke? Who the hell are you people?"

As Sam tries to close the door I rush forward and slam against it with both hands. He stumbles back and the door swings open. Sadie screams, and I see a phone in her hand. I grab hold of the old man by his sweater and shake him. "Tell me! What did she mean by that? What don't I know?" I cock back a fist but the old man just smiles at me as if he enjoys being assaulted. "I don't want to hurt you but I will, you understand me?"

"Leave him alone!" Sadie screeches, lumbering toward me with a broom. "The police are on their way! You never lived here! You never lived anywhere!"

I release the old man as his wife swings the broom. It misses me by less than an inch. I back up, hands in the air. "What do you mean? Tell me. What don't I know?"

"Get out of here!" Sadie screams with the broom out in front of her and leveled like a rifle, her wig mussed and her clownlike features glaring at me. "You get the *hell* out of here!"

"Don't you get it?" the old man says, winded. "There's no help for you here, son."

Sadie opens her mouth and something black and thick slowly oozes out. Her wig, cockeyed on her head, reveals a small section of scalp that is nearly bald and covered in strange bumps that appear to be protruding pieces of bone, skeletal and gnarled fingertips frozen and jutting out from inside her skull. She reaches up and pushes her wig back into place as best she can.

"Blessed is the slayer," she says, slurring her words as a bloated black tongue—long dead—dangles from her bloody lips, "destroyer of all that is holy."

Stumbling away and back down the steps, I run for my car.

* * *

A storm rages in my mind, dragging me deeper into madness. I have no memory of driving but find myself in Braintree some time later, parked outside Cliff's office.

In a daze, I fall from the car and stagger across the sidewalk. A small group of young professionals laugh and chat as they pass by. I melt into their ranks, then wander out the other side and lean against the double front doors of the building. The day has turned gray and ominous, the wind still blowing, ushering winter closer and closer still.

Once through the doors, I cross the lobby to a bank of elevators. Visions remind me I never want to step foot in an elevator again, so I turn and instead take the stairs, hurrying as best I can to the third floor.

I've only been to Cliff's office once before, but locate it quickly, at the far end of a long hallway on a floor housing numerous public offices.

A modest number of cubicles fill the worn, drab room, a series of tall windows along the back wall providing a grimy view of the streets below. Cheap industrial carpeting covers the floors, and a low hum of quiet conversations hangs in the air.

A reception desk separates me from the cubicles, and along the wall to my left are numerous people—mostly women with young children—sitting in plastic chairs waiting for the next available social worker.

"Can I help you?" a middle-aged woman at the reception desk asks.

Behind her, I see Cliff step out from his cubicle as he finishes up with a young couple. He shakes their hands, then guides them toward me.

"Excuse me?" the receptionist says. "Can I help you?"

"I need to talk to Cliff for a minute," I tell her, waiting for him to notice I'm there. "It's okay. He's a friend of mine."

When Cliff sees me, I force what is probably an absurd smile and wave him over. He returns the smile and ventures out and over to me. "Hi," he says tentatively.

"I need your help."

Cliff's face registers concern. "What's up?"

"Can we go somewhere a little more private?"

"Sure," he says, nodding, "but can you tell me what's wrong first?"

"You've got to…" I bite my tongue to keep myself from breaking into pieces, and lower my voice. "You need to get me to a doctor or a hospital or something, I…I need help."

With a look of deep concern, Cliff glances around as if to be sure no one else is listening. "Okay, I—of course, I—do you need an ambulance?"

"An ambulance?"

"Well, are you hurt? What's wrong?"

I move closer. "Remember the things we were talking about before?"

"Before?"

"At O'Callahan's."

Cliff's eyes lack their normal familiarity, their usual recognition. He subtly steps back, closer to the reception desk. "If I can help you in some way, I absolutely will, but you've got to tell me what this is all about, okay?"

And just like that, I'm cold as a grave. "You don't know who I am, do you."

Cliff smiles uncomfortably. "I'm sorry, should I?"

This time I back away. The people in the chairs all stare back at me like I'm a freak. "We went to college together."

"No kidding? You went to—"

"We've known each other for years, Cliff. You're my best friend."

"Um…okay." He gives the receptionist a quick sideways glance, and she picks up her phone and begins dialing even before he's returned his attention to me. "Why don't you have a seat for a minute and we'll get you some help, all right? Would you like a cup of water? There's a cooler just down the hall and I—"

"Why are you doing this?" I ask, a tremor ripping through me.

Cliff again looks back at the receptionist. She whispers something into the phone, then nods to him.

"How could you…" My mind is dying as the rage rises again. "How the *fuck* could you not know who I am?"

"All right, you need to calm down."

"This isn't possible. What the hell is going on?"

"Lower your voice and calm down," he says, cautiously slipping by me. "We've called the police, do you understand? Now, why don't you come with me and we'll go outside and talk calmly and wait for them, all right? Then we can get you the help you need. No one's going to hurt you or give you a hard time. We're here to help, okay?"

As Cliff reaches for the door, the long sleeve of his shirt creeps up his arm. Where skin should reside there is only bone, blood and chunks of flesh dangling free, a raw glistening patch just above his hand that runs from wrist to forearm and disappears beneath the sleeve.

I push him out of the way, rip open the door and charge back into the hallway as the receptionist lets out a scream.

Running through the corridor, I can hear his shoes clicking the floor behind me as he follows. "Wait!" he calls out. "It's okay, just come back! Stop and let me talk to you!"

I hurl myself down the stairs, taking three and four at a clip and crashing onto the platforms between floors before barreling down the next flight. When I reach the lobby, I increase my speed and shoulder my way through the front doors with such speed I lose my balance and tumble onto the pavement.

The initial contact knocks the wind from me, and although my shoulder hits first, my ribs, back and knees throb with pain by the time I come to rest near the curb. Ignoring the pain, I scramble to my feet in time to see Cliff standing inside the glass front doors, staring at me as if in a trance. As if…*possessed*…

The moment that word drifts through my head, he begins to smile.

People on the street hurry by like specters, bodies distorted, faces hideous masks of horror and sacrilege, movements erratic, violent and not human, their dark prayers whispered backward in ancient tongues.

I can still see Cliff watching me through the smudged doors, scraping his fingers across his bald dome hard enough to draw blood that trickles down across his face and into his goatee as he laughs. His face and neck bathed in blood, Cliff's body begins to quake and shudder in the throes of seizure, his laughter now a horrible screech.

I turn away and look to the heavens, eager for God. Instead, I see gray sky streaked with bands of orange and red, a slowly dying sun bleeding out across pewter clouds and a ghostly mist disguised as the dreams of the lost, the hopes of the forgotten and the tears of the damned.

I should be terrified. But I'm not.

I've seen the rainbows in Hell before.

CHAPTER TWELVE

Like always, it's the car alarm that wakes me, although I'm not sure this time if I was ever fully asleep. Watching shadows on the ceiling, I reach blindly across the bed for Remy but she's not there. I roll over, pull the sheets and blankets to my face and breathe deeply. I can smell her. My God, even her scent is beautiful.

I crawl out of bed and wait. It doesn't take long.

Through the window, I see a sudden gust of wind disturb a gathering of leaves in the front yard. I watch as the leaves swirl to form a small funnel, whirling about and suspended a few feet above the ground like a mini tornado.

From the center comes a shadow, dark and vague, slowly rising from the mass of orange and brown leaves. A hooded being cloaked in black, arms extended out like a giant bat, its feet dangling in midair beneath it.

I want to run, want to scream, but I stand frozen in place, eyes tearing as the entity rises higher still, floating just inches from the other side of the glass, its eyes little more than burning embers against the backdrop of dusk and faint traces of surviving moonlight. Yellow feral eyes, slanted and oddly majestic, as if belonging to a demonic feline, blink at me, slowly.

One arm curls, the black shrouded sleeve engulfing the being's limbs sliding away to reveal a hand with fingers that more closely resemble talons. A single crooked claw extends outward, then curls back, beckoning me.

"No," I say, uncertain if I actually spoke the word or only thought it.

It's time, Zeke.

Others come from behind it, walking in an uneven line from the nearby woods. Moving closer, they take up position behind their leader. Dozens of glowing eyes pierce my logical mind, laying waste to any semblance of sanity I may have had left.

Whispers emanate from the others, chants I do not understand but that sound oddly familiar. I can hear them through the window as the things float closer. The one in the lead drifts so close its face becomes visible. The cracked, bloody pale skin stretched across its head appears as if it might split apart at any second.

Did you really think we wouldn't find you, Zeke?

"This is all a dream. You're not real."

You're the one living a lie, Zeke.

The chanting forms move closer, the volume of their whispered mantra growing louder, nearly deafening.

"Where's Remy?" I growl. "What have you done to her?"

Suspended outside the window, the creature watches but doesn't answer. Its vile black tongue tracks cracked and bloodless lips.

"If you hurt her, I swear to you I'll rip you to fucking pieces."

Yessss…

"I'll show you pain like you've never imagined."

That's it, use that anger, Zeke. Embrace it.

"What have I done?" I ask, the taste of my own tears clinging to the back of my throat. "What have I done to make this happen?"

The thing extends its arms and slowly descends. The others are coming now too, I can hear them moving through the walls and into the house. I can hear them climbing the stairs, their odd chanting growing louder, clearer as they draw nearer.

I turn away from the window and it's in the bedroom with me, standing right next to me, so close I can smell its rancid breath, feel it exhaling against me. "This is a nightmare," I manage. "I'm dreaming."

Yes, Zeke, but your dreams belong to us.

And then it shows me my dreams. Flashes of death and depravity beyond comprehension flicker like old film before my eyes.

You belong with us.

"No…stop it…make it stop…"

It's time, Zeke.

"I'm dreaming," I tell it. "I'm dreaming I've gone to Hell."

We all try, Zeke.

"My name is Cameron Horne!"

Once or twice, we all try to change our destiny, our very existence.

"This isn't my destiny. I have a life, the life I've always wanted. Why are you…why are you trying to take it from me?"

The demon grins, lips peeling back to reveal bloody gums and razor teeth.

"Tell me," I say, pleading with it now. "Please, tell me."

The perfect life…it's all a lie, Zeke…created and born in your own mind. The history and memories of parents who never were, a childhood filled with wonder and love that only exists in this world of deceit you yourself designed and produced. The perfect house, the perfect wife, the meaningful and righteous job…all of it lies. Did you really think that by willing it—by stealing it and riding on someone else's dying dreams—that would actually make it so? Didn't you know we would eventually find you?

The others are just outside the bedroom doorway now, their chanting gnawing at my guts like rats, their ghoulish faces twisted into impossible smiles of…affection?

Every bird leaves its nest but eventually finds its way home, Zeke. We've come to bring you back...back to where you belong, where you were born and where your real life is...your real family.

I back into a corner, wishing I could dissolve through the walls as they had and escape this madness. "What...What are you saying?"

The others move closer still, forming a half circle around me, their claws reaching out to touch me, but not to harm, to...to pet...to stroke...

We've come to take you home, Zeke. To the very place you ran from.

And in that horrible instant comes a recognition I had buried so deeply I'd hoped I would never again have to face it. The true nature of who I am. Of what I am.

What I have never wanted to be but can no longer deny in a dream world I've constructed, stolen and assumed as my own. A chance to be normal and happy, a chance to be good. A chance to be...human.

Welcome home, Zeke. Welcome home.

* * *

I want my life back.

It's not your life.

"Bad dreams," Remy whispers in my ear, her breath hot against my face, her arms holding my head tight to her chest as she rocks us slowly back and forth. "It's just bad dreams, sweetheart."

"No," I tell her softly. "They're not."

"It's a cycle," she says. "Life...Death...Good...Evil..."

I can feel my blood coursing through my veins, pulsing in my temples, dripping behind my eyes. Somewhere in the distance there is a horrific shriek, but it's not human. Metal... machine...screeching and crashing, twisting, glass shattering and then silence...awful deadly silence...

Shelly hides in the corner of my eye, holding Apollo in her

arms. She wears a skimpy black dress and knee-high leather boots. Her mascara is smeared, staining her face with wet black sticky lines, her lipstick hastily applied and well outside the lines of her mouth, her hair a rat's nest.

Apollo can never die.

"Don't look," Remy says, stroking my cheek with her fingers. "They're trying to frighten you. Don't look."

You belong with me and Apollo. Come home.

The cat's yellow eyes watch me, unblinking.

You ran away. You ran away and left me.

Shattered pieces of mercuric glass fall all around us like rain.

Our flesh slashed, bloody and littered with tiny protruding shards of broken glass, Remy and I hold each other tight one last time. She sings to me, and it sounds like a chorus of angels.

Hallelujah…Hallelujah…Hallelujah…

Shadows close, and Shelly and Apollo are swallowed into darkness as the singing slowly fades.

"Look at me," Remy says. Her voice cracks with emotion and desperation as tears of blood leak from her eyes. "Stay with me, baby. Stay with me, stay—look at me, look at me—stay—stay with me!"

"Can you see it?" I ask her, my voice weak, distant and no longer my own.

"See what, baby? What do you see? Tell me what you see."

The most beautiful light…there…just above the trees…

CHAPTER THIRTEEN

Mac stands at the edge of the tree line, watching the forest. The car alarm continues to wail as I cross the yard and join him there. He glances at me, then returns his gaze to the trees and offers me a cigarette. We smoke one together, passing it back and forth until it's spent.

"Are you ready?" he asks, dropping the butt to the ground and grinding it out with the toe of his boot.

"Does it matter?"

He shakes his head no as tears spill from his eyes, but oddly, he looks closer to peace than ever before. "Come on," he says, offering his hand.

I take it, and together, we slip through an opening in the fence and cross into the woods, moving between the trees as the sun rises on the horizon, shooting trails of early morning light that filter through the forest.

We've not gone far when I see other lights, artificial blue shafts sweeping through the forest in strobelike bursts, and I realize it's not a car alarm I've been hearing all this time, but a siren.

There are others here. I can't see them, but I can feel their eyes on us.

We stop a few feet from the end of the forest. Just beyond the trees lies a busy street. There has been a terrible car accident involving two vehicles, both of which are hideously mangled and smoking. Several cars have pulled over and numerous people are gathered around a body next to one of the cars. The siren I mistook for a car alarm belongs to an as yet unseen ambulance, the blue lights those of police cruisers that have just arrived on the scene.

Mac lets go of my hand. I don't want him to, but neither of us has a choice.

My name's McEnroe.

He looks at me and smiles a sad little smile.

You know, like the tennis player.

His nose begins to bleed. And then his eyes.

Only it's spelled a little different.

McEnroe...McEnroh...

Did you really think that by willing it...

Mac Enroh...Cam Horne...

...by stealing it and riding on someone else's dying dreams...

Cameron Horne...

...that would actually make it so?

As he leaves me in an explosion of glass and twisted metal, I close my eyes. When I open them, he's lying in the street surrounded by people I recognize. They're all there, standing over him, watching and talking and milling about. A stout blonde woman pushing a baby in a stroller hurries away. Roz stares down at him, horrified, a hand to her mouth as she mutters, "I... I'm sure things will work out." Dario paces about, hands on his head. Sue is on her cell phone, crying. Jeffrey and Isabella and Leigh and Wayne are there too...and a woman with light brown dreadlocks and tattoos stands nearby, watching, her face showing no emotion whatsoever. A filthy and disheveled homeless man hovers by the sidewalk, nervously picking at his long hair and mangy beard. Even Marianne is there, hands clasped before her and lips moving soundlessly in prayer.

And Remy…my beautiful Remy…so much younger somehow, and closer than the rest, she holds him in her arms, his blood smeared across her blouse and hands. "Mac," she pleads, "stay with me, baby. Stay with me, the ambulance is almost here, okay? Look at me—no, don't close your eyes, look at me—stay with me, baby, stay with me now."

I step back into the forest.

The light through the trees, that's what I remember most, that beautiful golden light. Lying on my back on the forest floor, I look up at those trees. Such beauty, it's like having sight for the very first time. I breathe deeply and smell the forest all around me as the golden sunlight warms my face.

And in that strange and astonishing moment, I see it all there before me, unfolding like a magnificent dream.

You may think I'm crazy. You may not believe a word I say.

But I remember it all.

That beautiful light bleeding through the trees…the last dying breaths of a sad young man who understood his destiny and my truth long before I did…and a moment in time when anything is possible amidst the break of dawn just beyond the forest…

"But that's not sunlight," I ask the shadow in the corner of my eye, "is it?"

It's fire.

Such horrific majesty…

The fires of Hell…

There, at the very end of the rainbow.

Welcome home, Zeke.

And then I'm just another crazy wandering the city, a dark figure huddled in a doorway in the rain, hands stuffed in my coat pockets, hood pulled up over my head to hide my face, a horribly distorted reflection in passing car windows. Unnoticed and biding my time across the street from a dingy old abandoned hotel. Full of empty corridors, long-forgotten dusty rooms and an old elevator, it waits just for me as I watch my fleeting empire of smoke and mirrors slip away to darkness. Hope swallowed by night...love devoured by hate...so much sand through my fingers.

They're waiting for you... They've been waiting so very long.

I cross the street and slip into the building.

Everything happens in an instant. A million memories and thoughts and feelings fire through me. Words, images, smells, touch, tastes...it's all there and all at once.

The elevator doors open, but there is no faceless operator. There isn't even an elevator, just a dark, vacant shaft.

And so we do battle, Paradise and I, because the abyss is my home, not by choice but by providence. I never had a chance. But nearly any caged animal will run given the opportunity, even when they know there is no real hope of escape. Because it is those few moments of freedom, those few wonderful moments they've never experienced before and never will again that give them joy when the shackles are snapped back in place. For a moment, just a moment, I had it all.

"Forgive me," I whisper, and spreading wide my arms, step into air.

As I fall, piercing the darkness, I close my eyes, and in one final act of defiance, remember what might have been, in a place where devils burn away like so many fallen leaves; a hopeless runaway—a rogue male—has his moment in the sun, and even ephemeral glimpses of deliverance turn the darkest pits of Hell into a kind of Heaven.

If only for a little while...

AUTHOR'S NOTE

Although the *Office of Public Safety and Security* is a real department in the Commonwealth of Massachusetts, my interpretations, definitions and execution regarding all matters (including procedures, characters, locales and situations relating to it) are completely fictional and solely my own creations, and are in no way meant to reflect an accurate or real portrayal of the department, those employed there, or the fine work they do on a daily basis for the people of Massachusetts. *Rogue* is loosely based on a short story entitled *Runaway*, which was originally published in 1999 in Issue #3 of the magazine *Deadbolt*. Thanks to publisher Jim Lay for publishing it and for believing in the premise all those years ago. The plan had always been to take the concept and turn it into a novel, and eventually, I was fortunate enough to have the opportunity to do so. Thank you to Shane Staley, Dave Thomas and everyone at DarkFuse for helping to make the original edition possible, and big thanks to Chris Payne and Jess Landry at Journalstone for giving *Rogue* a new home with this second edition. Thanks also to my wife, Carol, and to my family and friends. I was often less than pleasant while working on this piece, and although I know you're all used to it and realize how I sometimes get when writing a novel, I appreciate your patience nonetheless. And finally, my sincere thanks to my readers and fans all over the world for their continued enthusiastic support. Each and every one of you makes this not only possible, but worth it.

—Greg F. Gifune
Thursday, September 25th, 2013
(updated Friday, June 29, 2018)
New England. Night.

Greg F. Gifune is a best-selling, internationally-published author of several acclaimed novels, novellas, and two short story collections. Working predominantly in the horror and crime genres, Greg has been called "the best writer of horror and thrillers at work today" by *New York Times* best-selling author Christopher Rice, "one of the best writers of his generation" by both *The Roswell Literary Review* and horror grandmaster Brian Keene, and "among the finest dark suspense writers of our time" by legendary best-selling author Ed Gorman. Greg's work has been published all over the world, translated into several languages, received starred reviews from *Publishers Weekly*, *Library Journal*, *Kirkus* and others, is consistently praised by readers and critics alike, and has garnered attention from Hollywood. Two of his short stories, "Hoax" and "First Impressions," have been adapted to film. His novel, *Children of Chaos*, is currently under a development deal to be made into a television series.

His novel, *The Bleeding Season*, originally published in 2003, has been hailed as a classic in the horror genre and is considered to be one of the best horror/thriller novels of the decade.

Greg resides in Massachusetts with his wife, Carol, a few cats, and a dog named Dozer. He can be reached online at gfgauthor@verizon.net or on Facebook and Twitter.

www.ingramcontent.com/pod-product-compliance
Lightning Source LLC
Chambersburg PA
CBHW052133170626
46812CB00004B/1385